Spotlight

Spotlight

On the Runway

Melody Carlson

BOOK FOUR

ZONDERVAN®

ZONDERVAN.com/
AUTHORTRACKER
follow your favorite authors

ZONDERVAN

Spotlight
Copyright © 2010 by Melody Carlson

This title is also available as a Zondervan ebook.
Visit www.zondervan.com/ebooks.

Requests for information should be addressed to:

Zondervan, *Grand Rapids, Michigan* 49530

ISBN 978-0-310-71789-8

Cover design: Faceout Studio
Cover photography: Veer
Interior design: Patrice Sheridan, Carlos Eluterio Estrada, Tina Henderson

Printed in the United States of America

10 11 12 13 14 /DCI/ 22 21 20 19 18 17 16 15 14 13 12 11 10 9 8 7 6 5 4 3 2 1

Spotlight

Chapter 1

I never wanted to be famous. I know there are people, like my best friend Mollie, who probably don't believe me. Of course, that's because Mollie would absolutely love to be famous. Unfortunately, Mollie's acting career is on hold because her baby is due in about three months.

Since I *never* wanted to be a celebrity, I'm experiencing some real culture shock over what's happened since our show *On the Runway* became a real hit. According to our producer, Helen Hudson, we're one of the hottest reality TV shows running right now and sponsors are lining up. This is totally great news—and I am happy for my sister, Paige, because this is her dream. But I'm still not comfortable with all that comes with it.

My general dislike of the limelight is not because I'm some highly evolved Christian who is too holy and humble to want to hog all this attention. Paige's theory that my fame-phobia is a result of my poor self-image isn't exactly right either. In fact, I think my self-image is fairly normal. I mean, how many young women—or old women—look in the mirror and absolutely adore what they see? Well, besides Paige.

But honestly, I'm pretty much okay with my looks. And most of the time, despite having a drop-dead-gorgeous sibling, I'm thankful that God made me the way he did.

My discomfort with celebrity is basically selfish—I happen to like my normal life and I enjoy my privacy, and I'd rather fly beneath the radar of the paparazzi than be running from them.

I think being in Paris last month gave me a false sense of obscurity-security, because Paige and I were able to film our episodes and go about our daily lives with very little intrusion from the media. Of course, Paige was a little troubled by this.

"It's like no one even knows who we are," she said as we walked through the Charles de Gaulle International Airport unobserved.

"Or they just don't care," I teased. And, really, Paris is kind of like that—subdued and slightly aloof. I think Parisians, totally unlike Americans, aren't too interested in celebrity spotting.

But Paige seemed bummed. Her way to protest was to sport her newest pair of Gucci sunglasses, hold her chin high, and strut through the terminal like she was a real star. And I'll admit I noticed heads turn. I'm not sure they knew who she was, or cared, though: she is simply an eye-catcher.

Fortunately, for Paige, we were spotted and even photographed when we arrived at LAX the next day. By then I had on sunglasses too, but mine were to hide the dark circles beneath my eyes after a mostly sleepless night during the eleven-hour flight.

"Is it true that you and Benjamin Kross were vacationing together in France?" a reporter from one of the gossip shows asked Paige as we waited to spot our luggage in baggage claim.

Paige smiled and tossed her head. "We were with a number of interesting people in France," she said brightly. "Benjamin was there for a few days as well."

"What did you think about Benjamin's settlement with Mia Renwick's family?" the reporter persisted.

"I think it's really none of my business." Paige smiled.

"What about rumors that you and Dylan Marceau are engaged?" the other reporter asked next.

Paige laughed. "They are just that — rumors."

"But are you involved with Dylan Mar — "

"I think Dylan is a brilliant designer and he's a good friend."

Just then I spotted some of our luggage on the carousel, and I abandoned my sister to her adoring paparazzi in order to help our director, Fran, drag the bags off. Sure, we might be "famous," but we still carry our own bags. At least most of the time, anyway. Blake has reminded me more than once that his offer to carry my bags, do shoulder rubs and pedicures, run errands, take out the trash — or whatever — is still good if the show wants to take him along with us. So far I don't think the show is too interested in Blake.

Unfortunately, Blake's interest in the show doesn't seem to be going away. And way too often, despite me asking him not to, he wants to talk about it. So why am I surprised when he starts in after our fellowship group? Several of us, including Lionel, Sonya, and Mollie, decided to extend the evening by meeting at Starbucks for coffee, and I've just taken a sip of my mocha when Blake brings it up.

"Did you guys hear that Erin is going to London next month?" he announces.

"Yeah, and she's not even excited about it." Mollie rolls her eyes at me.

"It's not that I'm *not* excited," I protest. "It's just that we haven't been back from Paris for that long. And we're trying to plan my mom's wedding and —"

"Excuses, excuses ..." Mollie waves her hand. "You are off living the life and all you do is complain, complain."

I frown at her. "Really? Do I complain that much?"

She gives me a sheepish smile. "Well, I might exaggerate a bit. It's only because I'm jealous. I would so love to go to London."

"Me too," Blake chimes in.

Mollie makes a face at Blake. "But you already got to go with Erin to Paris, so if anyone gets to go to London with her, it should be me."

"FYI," I remind her, "Blake went to France with *Benjamin Kross*, not me." And, okay, I know I'm doing this as much for Lionel's sake as for Mollie's, since he already questioned why Blake made that trip. I'm not sure if he was jealous or merely curious, but it's a topic I try to avoid.

Things have been a little awkward with both guys since I returned from the trip and put the brakes on both relationships. As soon as I got home from Paris, I called both Blake and Lionel and told them the same thing: that Paige and I had made a pact not to date for a while and to focus on the show.

"Yeah, Erin didn't actually invite me." Blake turns to Lionel, almost like he's trying to get a reaction. "And when I got to Bordeaux, she already had a French boyfriend."

"You know that Gabin was *not* a boyfriend." I shake my finger at Blake. "He's just a good friend." We'd been over this several times already.

"Yeah, but he gave you that great bag." Mollie points to

my black Birkin bag, which has kind of become my signature piece of late. Not because it's such a fashion statement as much as it's really great for carrying my camera and junk.

"So what are you going to be covering in London?" Lionel asks me.

"Isn't it Fashion Week there?" Mollie suggests.

"Actually Fashion Week London isn't until September," I explain. "And the show will probably send us back to London then. This trip is to coincide with a new British TV show. It's kind of like *America's Next Top Model*. Paige is going to be a judge and we'll use that for an episode, then we'll do some episodes on the Brit fashion scene. And we'll stay at the May Fair and—"

"The May Fair is like the swankiest hotel in the coolest fashion district in London," Mollie explains. "I looked it up on the Internet and I was pea green with envy."

"And you're not excited about that?" Sonya asks me. She's been the quiet person in the group tonight. As usual, I wonder if she's still feeling a little out of sorts because of her breakup with Blake. And because she might secretly blame me for losing him, although I'd beg to differ. Sometimes I catch these glances from her and, despite Blake's assurance, I suspect Sonya isn't totally over him.

"It's not that I'm *not* excited," I say for the second time. Like is anyone listening. "It's just that—"

"Oh, admit it," Mollie pushes in. "You're like the heel-dragging, reluctant little starlet. Your TV show is handed to you on a silver platter and you turn your nose up and—"

"It was *not* handed to me," I protest. "It's Paige's show. I'm just a secondary character, if that. I'm the lowly camera girl and—"

"Not true," Blake interrupts. "That makeover episode in Paris sent your popularity soaring."

I frown at him. "And how do you know that?"

He grins. "Because I pay attention to these things."

"So do I," Mollie tells me. "And, whether you like it or not, that episode turned you into a star. So get over it."

Okay, now I don't have a response.

"I think they're right," Lionel confirms. "I saw that episode too, and I'm guessing that your role in the show is going to change."

"*Is* changing," Mollie interjects.

"And you're not happy about that?" Sonya looks like she'd love to slap me.

"It's just not what I wanted," I try to explain. "It's Paige's gig, not mine."

"Did you even listen to Eric's message tonight?" Blake demands with a twinkle in his eye.

I consider this. Eric is an assistant pastor at our church and he led the fellowship group tonight. But at the moment I'm blank. "I listened," I tell him. "But I'm having a hard time remembering . . ."

"Eric said that God sometimes puts us in bad situations for good reasons." Mollie grins at me like she thinks I'll give her a gold star.

"Oh, yeah." I nod. "Thanks, Mollie."

"Like Joseph," Lionel reiterates. "Sold as a slave by his brothers, then falsely accused and put in prison—talk about some hard situations."

"But God had a plan," Blake adds. "He worked it together for good."

I nod, knowing where this is going. "You guys are right. I do have the wrong attitude about the show."

"You need to see your TV show as an opportunity," Blake tells me. "You can be a light in a dark place, Erin. Remember that night in Bordeaux?"

"What night in Bordeaux?" Lionel asks with a creased brow.

I tell everyone about Blake's bonfire idea. "It's like everyone was starting to get into a big fight," I explain. "Our hostess was having some issues. Paige was caught in the middle. Yet somehow Blake managed to get everyone gathered around a campfire and we sang and stuff and then, before the evening ended, Blake actually gave his testimony and it was pretty cool."

Lionel actually gives Blake a fist bump. "That *is* very cool. Way to go, Blake."

Blake smiles and I can tell he appreciates this coming from Lionel. I must admit it's a relief to see a couple of Christian guys acting more like brothers than competitors.

"So maybe you need to remember Joseph next time you feel like complaining," Mollie tells me. "He didn't exactly like being sold as a slave or doing time, but he did his best and God used him in some big ways."

"And the bigger your role on your show becomes, the more visible you'll be," Lionel says. "And the more influence you'll have ..."

"To be a light in a dark place," Blake finishes.

And so that's my new attitude—or it's what I'm trying to adopt as my new attitude. I obviously need God's help to carry it off. But my goal now is to do my best job, and even if I don't particularly love being on the show, I'll give it my all and just see what happens. I thought that would make everyone happy—especially everyone working on the show.

Unfortunately, I quickly discover that might not be the case. The following week, after previewing a couple of the Paris episodes, Paige and I are in a planning meeting with Helen and Fran and the rest of the crew when Helen suggests that my role in the show has changed.

"I know that you like filming the show," she tells me. "But I see the show going a different direction now. We no longer need a camera girl."

"What do you mean?" Paige demands. "You can't take Erin off the show. I need her!"

Helen laughs. "No, of course we're not taking her off the show. *On the Runway* needs her too, Paige."

Paige has a relieved smile. "Oh, you scared me."

"Sorry." Helen pats her hand. "What I'm saying is that Erin needs to become more of a partner now."

Paige's forehead creases ever so slightly. "A partner?"

"Yes. No more remaining behind the scenes. The fans are connecting with Erin in a big way now. She needs to come out of the background and become a featured costar."

"A featured costar?" Paige looks unconvinced.

"Of course, you'll still be the host," Helen assures her. "But Erin will play a more significant and visible role alongside you."

"How, exactly?" Paige glances at me then back to Helen.

"Mostly by being herself." Helen smiles at me like I should get this. But frankly, I don't.

"We want Erin to bring her opinions about fashion onto the screen," Fran injects. "You two girls are so different. Sometimes it's hard to believe you're really sisters." She laughs. "But it's apparent that our fans are diverse as well. And we've gotten some great viewer responses in regard to topics like green design and economical fashion."

"So we've decided we need to include more segments along these lines," Helen finishes for her. "And Erin is the perfect one to take us there."

Everything in me wants to stand up and protest—to remind everyone in this room of our original agreement, that I am merely "Camera Girl" and that it's acceptable for me to remain a wallflower. But at the same time I remember the conversation at Starbucks on Saturday night. I remember how my friends challenged me to change my attitude and let God use me however he wants in regard to the show. So how do I back down now?

Paige lets out a little laugh then shakes her head. "Okay, I'll admit that *sounds* like a sensible plan and, naturally, we want to expand our audience. But there's one itty-bitty problem."

"What's that?" Helen adjusts her glasses and peers at Paige.

Paige makes what feels like a patronizing smile at me. "We all know how stubborn my little sister can be. Of course, Erin would never agree to this, *would you, Erin*?"

Now all eyes are on me, and with a furrowed brow Helen points her silver pen in my direction. "Is that right, Erin? Are you still going to play the spoiler?"

I clear my throat, which suddenly feels like sandpaper.

"Speak up," Helen urges.

"Actually ..." I glance at Paige then back at Helen. "I am actually ... sort of ... open."

Paige's jaw drops ever so slightly. "Open? Open to what?"

"Open to ... you know ... whatever. I mean, if the show needs me to step up, well, I'm willing."

Helen clasps her hands together. "I just knew you'd be game, Erin. I felt it in my bones. When I saw the initial footage from Paris I said to myself, our little Erin is finally growing up!"

Suddenly they're all talking and making plans, and it's obvious that they've already given this some serious thought, but when I glance over at Paige, who is sitting silently, I can tell she's not really on board. And the way she's looking is reminiscent of something ... something I'd nearly forgotten ... something that happened a long time ago.

When we were little—I was in kindergarten and Paige was in first grade—my sister begged my parents for gymnastic classes. Her friend Kelsey was bragging about how she was going to become an Olympic gymnast (which never happened), so Paige insisted she needed lessons too. My parents eventually agreed, but Dad decided both Paige and I should be enrolled in the academy so that I wouldn't feel left out. Naturally, I was happy to be included since I already loved jumping, climbing, and rolling around like a monkey. But after a couple of months at the academy, which I thoroughly enjoyed, Paige's interest started waning until she refused to go at all.

Years later, I learned by accident that Paige's reason for quitting gymnastics was simply because I'd been outshining her and she did not like to be second best at anything. Although I continued going for a while, it wasn't long before my sister convinced me that gymnastics was silly and the outfits we had to wear were even worse, and that it would be much more fun to take dance classes instead. Naturally, she turned out to be far more gifted and graceful at ballet than me. And, once again, she was back in her comfort zone—where she reigned.

Although my sister has grown up some since then — she's matured a lot these past few months, and our relationship is stronger than ever — I still suspect that some of her old habits die hard. Forcing Paige to share the limelight with me could come with its own set of challenges. Which brings to mind Joseph ... and how his own brothers sold him to strangers. Okay, I'm pretty sure my sister wouldn't sink quite that low. But it does give me pause to wonder.

Chapter

2

"*I know you'd hoped to find your bridesmaid* gowns in Paris," Mom says to Paige as we carry an assortment of dresses into the changing area of a new Rodeo Drive boutique that Paige insisted we had to try, "but it's so much more fun doing this together."

"I agree," I tell Mom as I head into a fitting room. "After all, it's your wedding. You should have a say in what we wear."

"And worst-case scenario," Paige calls from her room, "is that we have to get our dresses specially made. But I know a certain designer who might be willing to help us out ..."

I laugh as I pull the rose-colored satin dress over my head. "Yeah, I'm pretty sure Dylan Marceau would drop everything to make Paige a gown."

"Especially if I promised to wear it on our show," Paige says. "Are you ready yet, Erin?"

I strain to zip the fitted dress, then emerge from the dressing room, holding my hands out. "Ta-dah."

Paige presses her lips together then shakes her head. "Too boring."

I go over to the three-way mirror to see for myself. "I don't know. I think it's got potential."

"This one is much better." Paige strikes a pose in the lacy pale pink dress. Admittedly she looks pretty. But what else is new?

"It seems too frilly to me," I tell her.

"*Too frilly?*" She looks at me like I have dirt on my face.

I glance over at Mom, comfortably seated on the velvet-covered divan, and I can tell she's unsure. "I think you both look lovely."

"But which dress do you like better?" Paige asks as she struts back and forth like she's on a runway. "See how this skirt moves. And this delicate pink shade would look gorgeous in a garden wedding."

"But it doesn't really go with Mom's dress," I tell my sister. While Paige and I were in Paris, Mom found a two-piece dress at Neiman Marcus. It's an elegant ivory satin. Mom tried it on and fell in love with it and, despite her promise to let Paige help her with this, she impulsively purchased it. Paige acted like that was okay, but I could tell she wasn't too pleased. I suspect she's not overly fond of the dress or that Mom made the decision without consulting her. But I keep thinking, *this is Mom's wedding*—why shouldn't she get what she wants?

"Of course it goes with Mom's dress," Paige argues. "Almost anything would go with Mom's dress ... anything stylish that is." She frowns at my choice.

"This is stylish," I say. "It's a classic style and Mom's dress is a classic." I point at Paige. "That dress looks pretty on you, but it's too fairy-princess-like to look good with Mom's sophisticated dress."

Mom nods. "You know, Paige, I think Erin might be right."

Paige's expression looks like Mom just slapped her. "*What?*"

Mom points to my gown. "I'm not saying that dress is the exact right dress, but it would go well with my dress. They do have a similar style."

"As in boring."

Mom sighs. "Maybe some of us prefer boring, Paige."

"I'm sorry, Mom." Paige holds up her hands. "I think your dress is lovely. But I don't see why Erin and I need to mimic you. We can express a little more creativity than that."

"But it's Mom's wedding," I finally say. "Maybe she wants something more classic. Something timeless like pearls and roses," I suggest.

"Yes." Mom stands and comes over to where Paige and I are standing in front of the three-way mirror and nods. "I do like the idea of pearls and roses, Erin."

Paige is scowling now. "So suddenly Erin's the fashion expert. Is that what you're saying?"

"I'm not trying to step on your toes or diminish your gift of fashion sense." Mom shakes her head. "We all know that this is your territory. But perhaps Erin's style is more like mine."

"But Erin doesn't really *have* style," Paige says quietly. And, okay, maybe that's true. Or maybe it used to be true. Lately I've been trying harder; even Helen and Fran think I've come a long way. So why is my sister trying to pigeonhole me again?

I look at our reflections, the three of us, in the mirror. There's Paige, the tall, willowy, beautiful blonde — often compared to our handsome dad when he was alive, and more recently to a young Grace Kelly. And then there's Mom and me ... average-looking brunettes of average height with green eyes and even features. Can't Paige see the difference?

Mom, who's standing between us, slips her arms around

our waists and smiles. "Two beautiful daughters. I don't care what you girls wear to the wedding—I know it will be perfectly lovely."

And so, not wishing to cause any further ado, I go back to the fitting room and remove the rose-colored dress and try on the next. But it's horrible compared to the first one, and the third one is all wrong.

"I don't think this shop has what we're looking for," I tell Paige quietly. The saleswoman is hovering nearby nervously and I suspect she knows who we are, which is just one more good reason we decided to do a reconnaissance mission before allowing the show to film us shopping for bridesmaid dresses. We wanted to avoid pressure.

"Thank you for your help," Paige tells the woman politely. "We'll keep these dresses in mind." Then we gather our things and leave.

"So I think I understand what you want," Paige tells Mom as we walk down Rodeo Drive. "Do you have any objections to checking out Chanel?"

"Well . . ." Mom sighs. "I would prefer to stay within our budget."

"But if we do the wedding episode, Chanel might be within your budget." Paige pauses in front of the Coco Chanel boutique. "We can at least look."

"You're right." Mom nods as she reaches for the door. "We can look."

"And if we like what we see here, we can ask Fran to speak to them and perhaps we can use their boutique in our show."

As we walk through the boutique, I realize that I'm not nearly as irritated as I used to be when Paige would drag me to shops like this. It's not that I enjoy it exactly, but after being in Paris and experiencing the language barrier combined with some of the Parisian attitude, I don't find Rodeo Drive nearly as intimidating as I used to. Naturally, the salespeople recognize Paige, and as soon as she lets our intentions out of the bag, we become the center of attention—the manager even offers us wine and chocolate.

"We only want to look today," Paige explains. Then she tells the manager that our mom already purchased her dress and we now need to find something compatible. "Something classic and timeless," she says, using my exact words, "that would go well with pearls and roses."

And, okay, I'm trying not to gloat here, but maybe I'm not as fashion-challenged as my sister would like to have me think. As it turns out, Chanel has some good, albeit expensive, options. The manager even offers to have a few more things sent to the store that we might like to consider when we return.

Paige gives her a business card and promises that someone will call to see about setting up a show. "Of course, we wouldn't want to do it during normal business hours," she tells her. "We don't want to disrupt your regular customers."

"I'm sure we can accommodate your needs," the woman assures her.

"Well, I think we're on the right track," Mom says as we walk down Rodeo Drive. "And, really, hasn't this been fun?"

I'm thinking "fun" might be overstating it a bit. But I try to maintain my party face as we walk over to the restaurant where Mom had made late-lunch reservations. Fortunately, Paige seems to have forgotten our earlier disagreement, and she tells Mom another amusing story about something that happened in Paris.

"It's hard not to be jealous," Mom says when our salads arrive. "But Jon has promised me that we'll go to Paris sometime."

"Why not for your honeymoon?" Paige suggests.

"I'd rather go in the fall or spring," Mom tells her. "Besides, Jon is looking into an Alaskan cruise."

Paige makes a face. "Really? That is what you'd want to do?"

Mom smiles. "I think it sounds rather nice . . . and relaxing."

"Not to mention beautiful. I'd love to do something like that just for the photo opportunities alone."

"Not me . . ." Paige gets a dreamy look. "If I were going on a honeymoon, I'd choose a location like Paris. Or maybe somewhere in Italy . . . like Tuscany . . . or maybe even the Riviera."

"Maybe Eliza will let you use her place," I tease.

Paige gives me her exasperated look. "Yeah . . . right."

"And if you were taking a honeymoon somewhere on the Riviera," Mom persists in this line of craziness, "who might you be taking it with?"

Paige laughs. "Oh, that's undetermined."

"So you don't see either Benjamin or Dylan in that picture?" Mom's tone is hopeful.

I watch Paige's reaction. She and I talked about this very thing on our last night in Paris. Maybe it was because I'd surprised her with the Birkin bag, but Paige turned very sisterly that evening. And during a heart-to-heart about our recent relationships, we both decided we weren't in a good place to be seriously involved with guys right now. As I recall we agreed to put the show ahead of romance. We both felt there's enough drama without adding more of our own in the area of romance. At least that's how I remember it.

But now Paige almost looks like she's in another world — as if she's imagining herself honeymooning with someone, like Dylan or even Benjamin, on the Riviera. "Oh, you never know," she says mysteriously to Mom.

Mom sort of laughs, but I can tell she's uneasy with this response. I simply stab my fork into my salad and realize that when it comes to Paige and matters of the heart, I probably should not trust my sister too much.

Paige excuses herself from lunch early. She doesn't say why or where she's going, but since we came in separate cars, it's not really a big deal.

"Do you think she's seeing Benjamin?" Mom asks me as we share a piece of lemon cream pie and coffee.

"I don't know," I admit. "The truth is, I've been wondering."

"Paige didn't tell me too much about his unexpected visit to France ..."

I give Mom the nutshell version of how Eliza subversively invited Ben, and how he surprised everyone by showing up with Blake in tow. "I know Eliza's reason for inviting Ben was to distract Paige from Dylan. But it seemed like Paige kept both guys at a distance. And when Dylan returned to New York, I got the impression that he wasn't too happy about it."

"Meaning he wanted to be more involved with Paige?" Mom scoops some of the meringue off the top of the pie with her spoon.

"That's what I suspected. And Paige seemed to confirm it by telling me that she didn't want to be seriously involved with anyone." I frown down at my coffee. "In fact, we kind of made a pact."

"A pact?" Mom looks surprised.

"To keep our romantic lives on hold ... you know, so we could focus on the show better."

Mom smiles. "Perhaps that's easier said than done."

I nod. "And when Benjamin showed up in Paris a couple days later ... it was the night before he was going home and Paige went to dinner with him ... and now I'm starting to wonder."

"If they're getting back together?"

I shrug. "I don't know."

"What about you and Blake?" Mom persists. "Did you go to dinner with him in Paris too?"

"No ... Blake had to go home a couple of days before Ben. He had classes and stuff."

"Smart boy."

"I guess. He's been smart not to pressure me too much about our relationship. I kind of told him that I was taking a break for now."

"Because of your pact with Paige?"

I consider this. "Maybe. Or maybe I think I need a break."

Mom chuckles. "Smart girl."

"Why?" I study her.

"Oh, it just sounded like you were getting in a little over your head."

Okay, now I sort of regret confiding in Mom after I got home from Paris. I told her a little about Gabin and Blake and Lionel and how weird it was to have three guys semi-interested in me at once.

"You're only eighteen," Mom continues.

"Almost nineteen," I remind her.

She smiles. "Yes. And a mature *almost nineteen*. But I still think you're wise not to get too involved right now. Take your time."

I nod as if I agree. And, actually, I *do* agree. Yet there's something about my mom telling me to *take my time* that makes me want to do just the opposite. Unreasonable, yes. But it's true.

Mom glances at her watch. "Well, as delightful as this has been, I've got to get back to the station."

"And I have an appointment with Helen at four thirty," I tell her.

"That's kind of late in the day for an appointment."

"It was last minute. She called this morning."

"So you're meeting Paige there?" she asks as she signs the check.

"Paige isn't going."

"You mean just you and Helen are meeting?"

I suddenly realize that I never really told Mom about Helen's new plan to make me Paige's costar. The truth is I've been avoiding this sticky subject, especially when Paige is around. But I realize that Mom will hear about it sooner or later. So as I drive her back to the station, I give her a quick rundown.

"Oh, that's wonderful, Erin," Mom exclaims. "I can understand Helen's thinking — that's a great plan."

"I guess." I let out a frustrated sigh.

"But you're still reluctant?"

"The funny thing is that I'm actually willing."

"So what's the problem?"

I glance at her and wonder why she doesn't know the answer to her own question. But then, when it comes to Paige, my mom can be a little dense sometimes. It's like Paige is her blind spot. Once again, I miss my dad. I have a feeling that if he were alive he would totally get this. "The problem is" — I try to think of a good way to say this — "Paige."

Mom nods. "Oh . . . is Paige reluctant to share the stage?"

"What do you think?"

Mom laughs. "I think you have your work cut out for you."

I'm pulling into her station's parking lot now, maneuvering my Jeep toward the entrance to drop her off.

"But if anyone can make this work, you can, Erin."

I frown at her. "How's that?"

She taps the side of her head with a knowing smile. "You'll figure it out."

"I hope so."

"Thanks for the lift," she tells me as she gets out.

"And thanks for lunch."

"By the way, I really did like the bridesmaid dress you picked out." She winks at me. "And Paige is coming around too."

I nod and wave, watching as my mom hurries into the building. Not for the first time, I consider the dynamics among the three of us — Mom, Paige, and me. I realize that I'll never completely figure out what it is about Paige that makes Mom treat her the way she does. It's kind of like she's protecting Paige. I guess, to be fair, I've learned to do pretty much the same thing. But sometimes . . . I wonder, *is it a good thing?* Or are Mom and I simply allowing Paige to get away with being a brat — she throws a tantrum and we turn our heads and look away, almost like a form of enablement? And yet, Paige is Paige . . . even when she's acting spoiled, most people seem to still love her. And, according to Helen Hudson, Paige's fan base just keeps growing, so why would Helen want to change anything about her? Of course, Helen doesn't have to live with my sister. Even if she did, she might eventually discover, like Mom and I have, that it's a lot easier to let Paige have her way.

Someone behind me honks, and I realize I'm still parked in the loading zone by the news station. As I pull out into traffic, I decide that I'll probably never fully understand my sister.

Chapter
3

As I drive through town, my phone rings and, seeing it's Mollie, I pull into a handy parking lot to answer it. "What's up?" I ask, knowing that with Mollie it could be anything. Her hormones combined with her broken heart are playing havoc with her emotions lately.

"Where are you?" she asks in a slightly desperate tone.

"Uh ... Seven-Eleven."

"*Why?*"

"Because I just pulled in here to answer the phone."

"Where are you going?"

So I tell her about wedding shopping with Paige and Mom and how I'm on my way to meet with Helen Hudson.

"Meaning you don't have time to talk?"

I glance at the clock on my dash. "Actually, I do have time. What's going on?"

"I don't think I can do this, Erin."

"Do what?"

"Have this baby."

"But ... you're like six months pregnant, Mollie. You need to have the baby—"

"I don't mean the giving birth part. I mean I don't think I can keep it and raise it." She starts to sob and I don't know what to say. What in life prepares someone to counsel her best friend about being a single mom?

"So what brought this up today?" I ask a bit helplessly.

"I saw this real estate commercial on TV," she sobs. "This family—a dad and a mom and two little kids and a dog. I just fell apart."

I'm trying to wrap my head around this. "A TV ad upset you?"

"Yes—they were a *family*, Erin," she cries. "*They were buying a house!* Don't you get it? I will never be able to do that. My child and I will be destined for—for poverty."

"Oh ..." I try to think of something comforting. "A lot of single moms make it, Mollie."

"I'm not strong enough to parent this child alone."

"Then maybe you need to rethink this, Moll ... I mean, maybe the baby needs a different kind of home."

"You're telling me to give my baby up?"

"I don't know." Okay, now I know I've stepped over the line. I also have an overwhelming sense of déjà vu; this is what happened the last time Mollie and I talked about the baby.

"You're just like my parents, Erin. And everyone else for that matter. Why is it that *no one* encourages me to keep my own baby? *Why?*"

Talk about being caught between a rock and a hard place. Didn't *she* just say she can't do this—can't be a single parent? Really, what am I supposed to tell her?

"Sorry I bothered you," she says finally. "I just thought my best friend would have something more encouraging to say."

"Fine. I do have something to say."

"What?"

I take in a deep breath. "Okay … you need to take this one day at a time, Mollie. You need to kind of step back and take care of yourself, and your baby, and you need to trust that God will show you what to do next. Remember he promises to give us what we need for today. *Just today.*"

"Okay …" She sounds a little calmer now.

"Okay."

"So why didn't you just say that in the beginning?"

I control the urge to yell that I'm not a trained therapist and that I'm doing the best I can here. "And, one more thing."

"What?"

"You need to stop watching commercials like that."

She actually kind of laughs, which is a relief, like she's crawled in off the ledge now.

"Seriously," I add. "Some ads are psychologically designed to trigger an emotional response. You should see my mom when this particular coffee ad comes on. She's like a basket case."

"Okay. I'll just say no to commercials."

"That's right." I look at the clock again. "And I need to go talk to Helen now."

"So what's up? Something new with the show?"

I realize I haven't told Mollie my latest news, and so I promise to give her a full update later. She begs me to stop by her house on my way home.

"Okay," I tell her. "It'll probably be close to six by then."

"That's okay," she says quickly. "It's not like I have a life anyway."

As I drive to the studio, I consider how much of a life I have — or don't have. Besides work, it seems that most of my spare time has been spent with Mollie. I realize she's in a very needy place right now, and spending time with her has been good overall. I know that I promised to be a better friend to her, but sometimes I feel selfish — like I should be able to do what I want to do.

The truth is I actually miss Blake. I miss his phone calls and going out with him. And, to be honest, I miss Lionel too. I'm starting to wonder if this so-called pact with my sister wasn't just a figment of my imagination. Or perhaps it's one more way for Paige to keep me under her thumb while she goes out and does whatever she feels like, even if it's a huge mistake — so that I'll be available to pick up her pieces. And what would happen if I blew my life to smithereens and she was the one who had to clean it up?

"Sorry to call this meeting at the last minute," Helen tells me after her assistant, Sabrina, tells me I can go into her office.

"That's okay." I sit down in one of the leather chairs and wait.

"Did you tell Paige we were meeting without her?"

"It's not like I purposely *didn't* tell her," I admit. "But it just never came up."

"How did the bridesmaid dress shopping go?"

I roll my eyes then laugh. "It'll probably make a good show. Paige wants to film it at the Chanel boutique and the manager seemed to be game."

"Of course she's game. It's free advertising."

"Right." I wait, wondering exactly why Helen didn't want Paige here this afternoon.

"You've probably guessed why I wanted to keep this meeting private today?"

"I suspect it has to do with Paige's attitude about having me as her new costar on the show."

Helen nods with a coy smile. "Yes … you and Paige are both smart girls. But you have a different kind of smarts. Paige is sharp and savvy when it comes to fashion, and has wit and charm. In fact, the girl is amazingly gifted."

"I know."

"But you seem to have a gift of empathy and a sense of reality that our viewers love too, Erin. And that's no small thing."

I kind of shrug. "Thanks."

"The question is how to get both of you girls on the screen without shutting Paige down. That's why I've invited you here today."

"Okay …" I nod. "I get that."

"For starters, I want to say that your opinions matter to the show, Erin."

"Right." I realize she's perfectly serious, but I almost want to laugh since my opinions have never been much of a consideration before.

"I've observed you in the past, at our planning meetings," she continues. "I've seen that glazed-over expression you get, as if you couldn't care less what we do or don't do. I know that fashion is not your thing."

I hold up my hands helplessly. "Hey, Paige is my sister. She's the expert. That doesn't leave much room for me in that arena."

She adjusts her glasses, narrowing her eyes at me. "And yet I think you understand it a lot more than you usually let on. It's as if you are so used to taking the backseat when it comes to Paige that you don't even try."

"I'm sure that's partially true. But it's also true that I'm not that into fashion. There are two main reasons I've stayed interested in the show." I hold up one finger. "First of all, because I do care about my sister, and both Mom and you felt she needed Jiminy Cricket by her side. But to be fair, I think she's grown up a lot and that part of my role could be lessening." I hold up my second finger. "Secondly, my motivating reason is that working in film and TV was always my goal. So getting to be part of the camera crew has been a real education."

"Yes. But it's my opinion that to learn the most about TV and film, people should immerse themselves completely. That means experiencing all aspects of the industry. I believe the best directors are multitalented—behind the cameras, in front of the cameras, writing, editing, promoting . . . you name it and they can do it. Take Woody Allen, for instance. He's done it all and, in my opinion, he's brilliant."

I consider this. Woody Allen's not my favorite Hollywood example. "How about Charlie Chaplin?"

She nods eagerly. "Exactly my point. He acted, wrote, directed, produced—the works. The man was pure genius." She picks up a pen and shakes it. "And that brings us back to you, Erin. I want you to appreciate that you will learn more about this business if you'll take your role costarring with Paige seriously."

"I plan to."

She looks a bit surprised. "Really?"

"Seriously, I do plan to. I think it's a great opportunity. I already have a show I'd like to discuss with you."

"Really?"

"Remember how I wanted to do a show that focuses on models and body image and eating disorders and how all of this impacts the average American woman?"

She nods slowly. "Yes. I realize we ran out of time in Paris. But that's the kind of episode that can be filmed anywhere. Perhaps it's less offensive to the international markets if we handle it right here in Los Angeles anyway."

"That makes sense."

"So …" Helen presses her lips together. "I'm making an executive decision. I want you to take the lead in that show. Talk to Fran and do your research and we'll see how it plays out."

"Okay."

"But I also want you to help Paige with this transition, Erin. The last thing we want is for her to shut down. We need her to make the show work. No Paige … no show. And I have a feeling, since you've known her a lot longer than we have, that you probably have some basic understanding of how the girl works."

"Or at least some coping skills," I offer.

Helen laughs. "Yes, I'm sure none of us can completely comprehend how that pretty head of her's works. But, don't be fooled, it does work."

"Don't worry, I know that."

"And somehow you've got to do your best to make sure that you two work together." She gets a serious look. "I know that's a lot to ask, Erin. But I have a feeling you can deliver."

This sends a shiver of insecurity down my spine, but I put on a brave face. "I hope so."

"Good." She claps her hands now, her signal that we're done here. "So consider yourself officially promoted." She stands.

"So does my promotion mean I get a raise?" I ask hopefully.

Helen laughs. "Why don't you ask your agent to make an appointment with me? We can discuss renegotiating your contract."

I nod. "Okay. I will."

So on my way out to the parking lot, I decide to give Marty Stuart a call. Paige and I both signed on with Marty several months ago. Jon produces and co-hosts the *Rise 'n' Shine, LA* show and Marty is his agent too, and, although Marty hasn't done much more than negotiate our original contracts, he's a good guy.

"Hey, Erin," he says to me as if we're old friends. "What's up?"

I quickly fill him in on my meeting with Helen and how she suggested he contact her. "Do you think I was out of line to ask for a raise like that?" I finally ask.

He laughs. "Not at all. But it's my job to negotiate it with her."

"Oh, good."

"I've been thinking it's about time to renegotiate for both you girls. With the show's new level of popularity, the stakes are rising." He promises to get back to me and hangs up.

Feeling very much like an adult, I get into my Jeep and drive home. As I drive, I consider how I can make the episode about fashion and body image work for the show. For starters, I think I need to come up with a strong title—something that will grab viewers' attention and make them want to watch. I play with a number of ideas and finally decide on: "Killer Style: What Happens When Fashion Turns Lethal?"

Okay, it might be a little too extreme for our demographics, but it's a start. And, really, according to some of my research, a few models have actually died from complications of eating disorders. Plus, I know that millions of young women are affected daily by the images of super-thin models. The truth is I've struggled with my own body image as a result of the constant exposure to the beauty myth that *thin is so in*. Spending time in Paris and around some stick-thin models didn't help much either, although I try not to give in to that kind of warped thinking.

I recently read a statistic that most fashion models weigh about a fourth less than the average American woman. One-fourth less! I find that both astonishing and disgusting.

As I stop for a red light, I notice a billboard with yet another overly thin and scantily clad model holding a very expensive bottle of designer cologne and gazing at it as if she's in love with it, when in reality she's probably just wishing it were a milkshake. I have to wonder — why do we as a culture put up with this crud? And am I, by being part of a TV show about fashion, aiding and abetting in the degeneration of the mental health and well-being of the American woman? Okay, that's probably overstating it. But I have to wonder.

As the light turns green, I remind myself that Paige, while naturally thin, isn't of the anorexic variety. She does seem to respect health issues. Also, I tell myself, I will do what I can to reeducate our viewers. If that's even possible. I sigh as I envision the image of the little Dutch boy sticking his finger in the wall of the dike in order to hold back the floodwaters threatening the entire town. This won't be easy.

Chapter
4

"*What's so interesting?*" *Mollie asks as she* returns to the family room with a pizza box in hand. We started watching an indie movie that Lionel recently recommended to me, but it's turned out to be kind of a bomb. So I've switched gears and am now plugged into my laptop.

"Research," I tell her.

Mollie drops the cardboard box onto the coffee table, something she would not do if her neat-freak mom were home, but since her parents are on a Mexican cruise right now, celebrating their twenty-fifth anniversary—a trip they booked almost a year ago and Mollie insisted they take—Mollie has let the house get pretty messy. "What are you researching?"

"In my new role as costar Helen is letting me put together a show about how fashion impacts the body image of the average American woman."

Mollie laughs sarcastically as she rubs her bulging, round stomach. "Probably not as much as pregnancy does." Thanks to her lime green warm-ups, combined with her red curly hair and short stature, Mollie reminds me of a chubby leprechaun today. Not that I would ever, in a million years, say this to her.

"Right ..." I look back down at my screen. "It says here that in a recent survey, twenty-seven percent of teen girls felt media pressure to have a perfect body."

"Only twenty-seven percent?" She frowns as she takes out a slice of pizza. "That seems pretty low to me."

I nod as I reach for a piece. "I know. But maybe not all the girls surveyed were honest. Think about it—no one likes to admit to feeling media pressure. But it's a well-known fact that most American women don't like their bodies. Where do you think those ideas come from?"

"From being bombarded with images of beautiful women ... probably starting with our first Barbie doll." She flops down on the sectional and turns off the TV.

"Exactly." I nod as I take a bite. "I never did like Barbies."

She laughs. "Not me. I *loved* my Barbies."

"Why?" I ask. "Why would you love something that made you feel like you didn't measure up?"

"Barbie was so perfect." With her pizza suspended halfway to her mouth, Mollie gets a dreamy look. "Those long slender legs and cute little feet ... those perky boobs—and now that I think about it, she never even needed a bra. And she looked fabulous in every outfit. Man, that girl could even make army boots look good." She sighs and takes another bite.

I control myself from throwing a pillow at her. "But how did that make you feel back then? More importantly, how does it make you feel now?"

"Fat." Mollie looks at her rounded belly with a slightly astonished expression, as if she can't quite believe it herself.

I try not to laugh.

"And short. And plain. And ugly." She sighs.

That makes me feel more like crying. "But that's all wrong," I tell her. "You are adorable, Mollie. Sure, you've gained weight because you're pregnant, but that's a temporary thing. Otherwise, you are petite and pretty, and your hair and coloring is stunning. You're a doll. And I don't mean a plastic one either."

She smiles at me. "Thanks."

I decide to google something. I've heard that Barbie's dimensions would be pretty strange if she were a real woman. "Listen to this," I say suddenly. "It says here that if Barbie were human she would be nearly six feet tall and weigh about one hundred pounds, which means she would be so grossly underweight that she'd have stopped menstruating and could never have children. Plus her nineteen-inch waist would have difficulty supporting her nearly forty-inch bust, which would probably result in serious back problems. And her feet are so small she probably wouldn't be able to walk."

Mollie shakes her head. "Poor Barbie."

"*Poor Barbie?* What about the poor American woman who will never be happy with her body because she's so stuck on the idea that she should look like Barbie? And yet the madness continues as these same women buy their little girls more Barbies. *What is wrong with this country?*"

Mollie laughs. "Lighten up, Erin. It sounds like you're suggesting we start a Barbie-burning campaign."

I ignore her as I continue to read more alarming statistics.

"Even if there were no more Barbies, there'd still be fashion models," Mollie persists. "I'll bet their height and weight ratios are almost as extreme as a human Barbie. I've heard of six-foot models weighing around a hundred and ten pounds. Walking skeletons."

"That's true." I nod and point to my computer screen. "But listen to this. Did you know that the average American woman weighs about one hundred forty-five pounds, wears a size eleven to fourteen, and is about five foot four?" I consider this. "Hey, that means I'm taller than average. Who knew?"

"And I'm almost average." Mollie sounds hopeful. "All this time I've been thinking I was short."

"According to this article, we've all been brainwashed by the media." I shake my head. "No wonder we obsess over our appearance so much. It's like we've been trained to measure our self-worth based on our physical looks."

"Pathetic." She wraps a string of cheese around her pizza and takes another bite.

I nod. "It really is. And, think about this, Mollie. You and I are okay looking. I mean, we don't have any serious defects or—"

"You mean besides my oversized stomach."

"You know what I mean. It's like we're relatively attractive. But what about other girls—ones who have serious challenges like obesity or physical defects or terrible acne—how do you think they feel?"

"Maybe they don't care."

I frown at her. "You think they don't care?"

"You know … maybe they just give up on the whole stupid beauty thing and get on with their lives, become doctors or lawyers or missionaries."

"In that case, they'd be the lucky ones. I could be jaded, but I seriously doubt that too many women in this country *don't care* about their looks. Or if they do, they're the exception." I continue skimming websites, gathering facts, and I realize that "Killer Style" is a show that *On the Runway* has a moral responsibility to do. "And get this," I tell Mollie. "The diet industry alone generates nearly fifty billion dollars a year. How is that even possible?"

"Because everyone wants to be thin." Mollie sighs. "Okay, you're depressing me now, Erin. The truth is I want to be thin too."

"Give it a few months."

But I'm actually depressing myself too. It's hard to believe how American women have been victimized by the beauty myth—that we're only worthwhile if we turn heads. It's like this faulty thinking has seriously handicapped us and impaired our reasoning. And in my opinion Los Angeles is particularly messed up. When I read about things like extreme dieting, bulimia, anorexia, plastic surgery, hair removal, implants, teeth caps, liposuction, and everything else ... I feel like it's hopeless.

I close my computer and think, once again, about the little Dutch boy with his finger in the dike. I can't remember how that story ended. Did he remove his finger and drown in the flood or what? Also, he only had a small hole to plug. The hole I'm seeing is more like Niagara Falls or Lake Meade. How do you stop something like that?

For the next several days I obsess over my research until it's almost all I think or talk about. By Sunday afternoon, Mollie is fed up. "Enough already," she tells me as we're finishing up lunch at the mall. We stopped here after church to shop for some maternity clothes, since Mollie has outgrown just about everything in her closet. "Did you even listen to this morning's sermon?"

I nod. "Yeah ... we can't change other people, we can only change ourselves. I get it."

"But"—she points her index finger in the air—"when we change ourselves, it can change the way we see others."

"Give the girl a prize," I tease.

"It was a good sermon."

"So what did it mean to you personally?" I ask.

She gets a thoughtful look. "I think it means that I need to quit focusing on Tony so much. I need to accept that he does not want to be a dad ... doesn't want to marry me. I need to let it go. Then I won't keep seeing him as ... well, as the devil."

I frown. "You see Tony as the devil?"

"Not literally. But sort of ..."

"Wow." I shake my head. "I didn't know that."

"I'm not exactly proud of it. But sometimes it feels like he got me into this mess ..." She holds up two tightly balled fists. "And then he runs off like a great big chicken ... and I get so angry that I'd like to seriously injure him."

"You should let that go, Mollie."

Her fists go back down. "I know. For the sake of the baby, I'm trying to forgive him, but it's not really a one-time-and-it's-done-with kind of thing."

"I can understand that."

"Well, hopefully by the time the baby comes, I'll have completed the process."

I smile at her. "I admire how grown up you're being, Moll. I'm sure I wouldn't do half as well if I were in your shoes."

"Speaking of shoes, I need to find some more comfortable ones since my feet seem to be getting bigger too. Mom told me that her feet grew two sizes when she was pregnant with me. Can you believe that?"

I just shake my head. And, no, I can't believe it. I wasn't exaggerating when I told her that I wouldn't handle it too well if I were in her shoes. I honestly don't know how she does it ... and more than that, how she will manage to do it when the baby does come. I cannot wrap my head around it.

So I'm determined to be the best friend I can to her. If that means picking out maternity clothes and sensible shoes, I can do that. But when Mollie begs me to go to the baby department to look at the cribs and things, I start to inwardly balk. I want to tell her to get real—I mean, she doesn't even know if she's keeping the baby! Why make things worse by looking at this stuff? And yet I manage to keep my opinions to myself.

"Isn't this adorable?" she says as she shows me her favorite nursery arrangement—turquoise blue baby furniture and magenta and lime green bedding.

"It seems kind of bright to me," I admit. "Do babies really like these kinds of colors?"

"I read that bright colors stimulate brain development." She runs her hand over the rail on the crib. "It's supposed to increase the baby's IQ."

"Oh ..." I wander over to a more traditional nursery setup with white painted furnishings and pale blue and yellow bedding. "I think I'd go more for this," I tell her. I pick up a teddy bear and pretend to rock it like a baby. "More soothing." Just then I feel someone watching me and I look up in time to see a teen girl pointing her phone at me with a triumphant grin.

"You're Erin from *On the Runway*, aren't you?" she calls from where she's standing with a woman I'm guessing is her mom.

I know I now have a choice—I can become indignant

and snarl at her … or I can smile and act nonchalant. Fortunately I have the good sense to go with the second option. She takes her shot and then I turn my attention back to Mollie as she comes over to look at the more subdued nursery set.

"Yeah … this is actually pretty nice. Much calmer." I hand her the teddy bear and she sighs. "I can't believe it's only three months away."

I press my lips together. No way am I going to stick my foot in my mouth right now. Especially with that teen girl close enough to overhear us.

"Mom told me I can move my bedroom down to the basement if I want." She gently sets the bear against the pillow in the crib. "I can make it into an apartment for the baby and me."

"Are you going to do that?"

"I don't know." She pats the bear's tummy. "I'm thinking about it."

It's so hard to respond. Although I want to be encouraging to Mollie, I don't want to encourage her to keep her baby, because I honestly don't see how she can manage to parent a child and finish school and have much of a life. But if I tell her how I really feel, I know I risk upsetting her. Best to keep my mouth shut.

So I keep my opinions to myself as we continue to shop. I chat about other things as I drive Mollie home from the mall, telling her about the plans for our next show. "Paige got Chanel to agree to let us film there while we pick out bridesmaid dresses." Then I tell Mollie about how Paige and I disagreed on what style would be best.

"No way." Mollie laughs. "You stood up to your sister's sense of style? Are you nuts?"

"But the dress Paige wanted would look weird with what Mom plans to wear. And it *is* Mom's wedding."

"But Paige *is* the fashion expert."

I consider this. "Yes. Paige is an expert when it comes to fashion. But maybe she's not the only one."

"So you're an expert now too?"

"Helen seems to believe in me." I hold my head higher. "And, sure, Paige and I have totally different taste. But maybe I've let her overshadow me too much. I mean, I know what I like. And I kind of know what looks good on me. Or at least I'm starting to figure it out. Admittedly, Paige has helped me with that some. But I also know what I don't like."

"Such as?"

"Such as expensive designer clothes. I honestly don't see why style has to be expensive."

"And you helped me find some good deals in maternity clothes," Mollie points out. "You actually found some pretty stylish pieces too."

"Thanks."

"So maybe you're right. Maybe you do need to step outside of the Paige shadow and let your own style shine."

"Yeah. That's what I'm thinking." I nod eagerly. "In fact, that gives me an idea."

"What?"

"I think I'll ask Helen if I can do my own kind of shopping spree for a show sometime. With cameras following me, I could gather up my own wardrobe of environmentally friendly and economically affordable threads—and do it with style."

"That sounds like fun."

"And I have some other ideas too. Maybe it's time to push

the envelope a little. How much *haute couture* can our viewers stand anyway?"

Mollie laughs. "Well, if they're anything like your sister, they will never tire of it."

"But what if their wallets are more like yours?"

Mollie nods. "Good point. You should go for it, Erin. I think you have some great ideas. By now you must know enough about how the show works to make some good pitches."

After I drop Mollie off, I go directly home and start putting together a plan for shows I'd like to pitch. The first episode is "Killer Style," and although I have gathered a lot of statistics and ammunition, I'm not totally sure how we would shoot it. I do know I would like to interview some models, hopefully ones who've been through some body-image struggles but who aren't still suffering from eating disorders. Like Paige Geller — I'll bet she'd do an interview. That could give it a more positive spin. The next show I'm calling "Cheap Chic." It would be about economizing the closet — how big style doesn't need to cost big bucks. And the third show I'm calling "Haute Green" — about how high fashion doesn't have to harm the planet.

I think these are all good, viable ideas for *On the Runway* episodes, but at the same time I know Paige is not going to like any of them. Well, except maybe the body image one since she's already agreed to it. But I'm hoping that Helen and Fran will like them and agree to produce them. More than that, I'm hoping that we can get a least one of them in the can before it's time to go to London. I'm also hoping that I can actually carry this off. I realize that means I need to get comfortable in front of the camera. I need to exude more confidence. And to do that, I think I need to practice.

Ideally, I would approach Paige and ask her to coach me. But I doubt that either one of us is ready for that. I consider asking Blake for help—I'm sure he'd be willing and probably even be good at it—but it kind of goes against my keep-the-guys-at-a-distance policy. Not that I plan to maintain this "pact" indefinitely. But I guess I want to do it just long enough to prove to my sister that it is actually doable.

Finally, I decide to ask Mollie for some assistance. After all, she seemed interested, and the distraction might be nice for her. Plus, she's taken a number of acting classes and knows how to run a camera. I simply hope it doesn't set her up to think she's part of the show or cause her to feel jealous. I don't want that. But, to my relief, she seems genuinely pleased when I call and explain my idea—and she's still enthused after I clarify that she won't be an actual part of the show. "It's more about getting me ready to take on a bigger role," I say. "Like an acting coach."

"Sounds like fun. I'd love to help," she eagerly tells me. "When do we start?"

"As soon as you want."

"I've got an idea. How about if you come over here and help me move my bedroom stuff down to the basement? Then we can use that as our studio since it has more room."

I gladly agree and we decide to go ahead and get started tomorrow afternoon. Mollie promises to study some of the previous *On the Runway* episodes in order to determine what it is I really need to work on. And I'll bring my camera equipment so we can critique my performances.

Whether this will work or not still remains to be seen. But at least it won't be as embarrassing or painful as it would be if I were doing it with Paige on an actual set. The worst-case scenario is that the practice doesn't help, and I tell Helen Hudson that she needs to rethink the whole costar plan. But the truth is, I actually hope it does work, because I think the episodes I want to do are both interesting and necessary.

Chapter
5

"*I wonder if you should be moving heavy things,*" I say to Mollie. We've just started to dismantle her bedroom and I'm beginning to have second thoughts.

"Oh, it's probably okay." She sets a drawer full of folded T-shirts on her already-crowded bed, then stoops down to pull out another drawer.

I watch her hunched over as she tugs on the bottom drawer, which seems to be stuck, and wonder what I'd do if she suddenly went into premature labor or, even worse, tumbled down the steep basement stairs while carrying down a piece of furniture. "What would your mom say?"

She shrugs. "Mom's not here, remember?"

I glance around her jam-packed bedroom, the same room she's had her whole life, and it's showing its age. Last year, her design goal in this room was to create "shabby chic," but I think she struggled with the chic part. "You know, Mollie, I think we need to make some kind of a plan."

"A plan?" She frowns up at me.

I bend down and help her dislodge the stubborn bottom

drawer, which is stuffed with old jeans, and I set it on the bed.
"Yeah. A plan. For starters, let's check out the basement and
decide where things are going to go down there so we only
have to move them once. Okay?"

She nods. "Yeah, that makes sense."

But once we're down there, I realize we need more than
just a plan. We need some Merry Maids. "This place is kind
of a mess," I say to Mollie as I pluck a string of cobweb from
her hair. "I can't believe your mom wants you to live down
here."

"Well, since they moved the laundry room upstairs, she
never comes down here anymore. I guess she doesn't clean
down here too much either."

I nod. That seems fairly obvious.

"It's kind of depressing, isn't it?"

I nod again. "That wall color doesn't help much." It's sort
of grayish beige. Maybe it's greige.

"I remember when Dad threw a bunch of leftover paints
together and mixed them up to get this."

I look down at the carpet, which is also beige and in need
of a good cleaning. Then, against the wall, there's a beige
couch and matching beige chair. "This place is like a sea of
beige," I tell Mollie.

"Pretty dreary, huh?"

"You're sure you want to do this?" I peer at her curiously,
thinking that her overly crowded bedroom is starting to look
a whole lot better.

"My parents kind of want me to move down here," she says
quietly. "I think it's so they can pretend this isn't happening."

"You mean the baby?"

She nods with sad eyes. "Dad's kind of in denial. I think

he's hoping that my pregnancy will be like a bad case of the flu ... it'll eventually just go away."

My heart hurts for Mollie, but I don't know what to say.

"And my mom is planning to turn my room into her office," she continues. "She thinks she's going to start writing a book."

I look around the dreary space, trying to imagine some way to make it more habitable. "What if we painted the walls a more cheerful color?" I suggest.

Mollie brightens for a moment and then shakes her head. "That'd be nice, but according to my pregnancy book, I'm not supposed to breathe paint fumes. It's bad for the baby."

"Yeah, that makes sense." I look around the room more carefully now and I suddenly begin to imagine it differently — like after a makeover.

"It's hopeless, isn't it?" Mollie goes over and sinks down onto the couch, and I can see the dust fibers floating through the dim light that's coming through the high, dingy window.

"No." I shake my head. "It's not hopeless at all. In fact, I'm starting to get a vision."

"A vision?" Her brow creases. "Huh?"

"Do you trust me?"

"Trust you to do what?"

"Makeover this room."

She laughs. "I don't think you could make it any worse than it already is, Erin. Sure, I trust you. What's your vision?"

"Well ... I'm still working on it. But you could start running a vacuum down here while I go check into some things. Okay?"

"Okay." She stands up with a slightly hopeful expression. "You really trust me?"

She smiles. "Actually, I do. Your room is pretty cool and you've always had a better sense about stuff like this than me."

"Are you still into shabby chic?"

She shrugs then makes a sheepish smile. "When it's done right."

"Okay ... I'm going to go pick up paint and a few other things while you do some cleaning down here."

"Do you need some money?"

"We'll figure that out later." Then I head out and, hoping that I'm not biting off more than I can chew, drive over to the closest home improvement store, where I find a color called sea glass green. The guy tells me he can mix it in the low VOC kind, which makes it safer for Mollie's baby. So, remembering that Mollie has always liked green, I decide to go with this peaceful shade of pale blue-green. While the guy's mixing it, I look around thinking *shabby chic ... shabby chic ...* And yet nothing in this store really seems to fit.

But then I see a pile of rugs on sale, and one of them reminds me of a rug in my grandmother's house—a braided rug her mother had made out of old fabric. This rug, though not handmade, is still interesting. Its soft shades of blue, rose, and green would brighten up that blah beige carpet. Then, after it's rolled and loaded onto an oversized cart, I head back to pick up the paint. But on my way, I pass by the outdoor furnishings and spot a set of white wicker chairs and a table marked fifty percent off. However, I realize there's no way those will fit in the back of my Jeep Wrangler.

That's when I call Blake, who has just finished his last class of the day. I explain my dilemma, the dreary basement, and how I want to help Mollie. The next thing I know, he's offering to borrow his dad's pickup and help me out. Blake arrives as I finish paying for this stuff, which is relatively cheap.

"Do you need some help with the painting?" he asks as we load things into the back of his dad's truck.

"Sure," I say eagerly. "That'd be awesome."

"I could call some guys from church," he suggests. "We'd finish it really quick."

"Great." I glance at my watch. "I have to make a couple more stops, but maybe you can head over to Mollie's now— I'll meet up with you in an hour or so."

"Will do."

"And don't let Mollie down there while you're painting," I say as he's getting into the cab. "Paint fumes are bad for the baby."

He nods. "Gotcha."

Next, I go to the discount fabric store across the street. I honestly don't know what I'm looking for, but I do have the pale green paint sample with me. Again, I'm thinking *shabby chic . . . shabby chic*. I'm also thinking I need to hurry. That's when I notice a table of decorator fabrics that are marked down to twelve dollars a bolt. A woman explains that they're the ends of discontinued bolts but promises they have at least six yards of fabric on each. So I grab a fairly heavy bolt of pale green and white stripes, a bolt of pastel plaid, and a bolt of multicolored pastel polka-dots. As I purchase these bolts, I have no idea how I'll put them to use. Mostly I want something to transform the ugly beige sofa and chair as well as to create cushions for the wicker chairs.

Finally, I stop at my favorite import store. I'm not even sure what I'm looking for exactly, but I'm hoping for a few items that will cheer up the basement. I stick to my pastel color scheme and emerge from the store with some lamps, a large watercolor print that I think Mollie's going to love, a soft pink throw, and some candles and other accents. As I drive toward Mollie's house, I'm becoming more and more excited at how cool that basement could end up being. At least that's what I'm hoping for.

I carry some things down to the basement to discover that Blake's paint crew consists of Blake and Lionel. As surprised as I am to see Lionel there, I'm thankful for his willingness because there are a lot of walls to paint. I put the bolt of striped fabric on the couch and think maybe it can work. Then I take the other bolts of fabric upstairs to Mollie. Fortunately, she knows how to sew and seems to understand as I explain my general plan to make seat cushions for the wicker and some pillows. "But you are banned from the basement," I firmly tell her.

"I told the guys I'd order some food," she says as she rolls out some fabric, smoothing her hand over it. "I like this."

With that encouragement, I head back down to the basement to attack the couch and chair, which I plan to "slipcover" with the help of scissors, a lot of strategic folding, and a big box of safety pins.

"You guys are doing a great job," I tell them. "The paint looks awesome."

"This is some really good paint," Blake says as he dips his roller into the tray.

"The guy promised me it would cover in one coat," I tell him.

Lionel nods. "It's a real time saver."

By the time we break for dinner, the basement is about two-thirds finished, and the section where I want to start arranging furniture into a living space is completely done. But when Mollie begs to see it, I tell her to forget it. "You can't go down there until tomorrow." I plan to spend the night to make sure she doesn't—and to make sure I complete this project.

The guys finish up the painting around ten. "Thank you so much," I tell them. "I think this is really going to encourage Mollie."

Blake looks around the room. "Yeah, it's a huge improvement."

Lionel nods over to where I'm now setting up the living area. "Looks like you have a knack for this, Erin. Maybe you should take some set design classes when you come back to UCLA."

"That'd be fun."

"You mean *if* she goes back to school," Blake teases. "From where I'm sitting, Erin's got a pretty good setup without college."

Lionel looks skeptical. "But that gig won't last forever."

"You're right," I tell him. "It won't." I thank them both again and invite them to come back tomorrow if they want to see the finished product. But I'm barely back to work when I hear their voices again.

"We thought we should move Mollie's bedroom stuff down while we were still here," Blake tells me. "Those stairs are kind of scary."

It takes them less than an hour to finish, and I go up to check on Mollie, who has now taken over her parents' bedroom. I can't help but laugh when I see her parked in the middle of their king-sized bed with a bag of microwave popcorn. "Oh, if your mom could only see you now," I tease.

Mollie laughs. "Yeah, she'd have a fit. But don't worry, I'll clean it all up before she gets home. She'll never know."

"I'm going to keep working downstairs," I tell her.

She frowns. "It's kinda late, Erin."

"I'm spending the night."

"Oh." She pats the bed. "Feel free to join me if you like."

"Or I'll just sleep down there."

She makes a face. "Ugh. That sounds horrible."

"It's steadily getting better," I assure her.

And by the time I call it quits, it really is better. Much, much better. It's also around three in the morning when, feeling like a zombie, I put fresh sheets on Mollie's bed. Then I crash.

It's around nine when I wake up, and it takes me a moment to figure out where I am. Then I make the bed and putter around and finish up a few things. I finally look around the basement with a very pleasant sense of accomplishment. The striped couch and chair are actually pretty cool. I've combined some of Mollie's interesting antiques and things with the wicker chairs and cushions and some of the new accent pieces, and it really does look like shabby chic. And, with the windows being open all night, I think the paint smell is pretty much gone too. It's time, I decide, to bring in Mollie.

I actually blindfold her before I slowly and carefully guide her down the stairs and into the basement. "Ready?" I ask.

She nods and I remove the blindfold. But she just stands there. Without saying a word, she looks around. It's like she's not having any reaction. She just keeps looking and looking. Then she turns to me and I see there are two streams of tears pouring down her cheeks as she grabs and hugs me, sobbing, *"Thank you! Thank you! Thank you!"* Then she lets go and dances around the room exclaiming about everything and how much she loves it. Now *that's* the reaction I was hoping for.

"It's so amazing," she tells me. "I absolutely adore it. I could live here forever. My baby and me ... forever."

Okay, I'm glad she loves it, but I'm not so sure about that last bit. I mean, it's not that I don't want her to keep her baby, but I don't like feeling that I may have encouraged her to do something that's not in her best interests. Then I remind myself—only God knows what's in her best interests. I pray that he shows her what that is.

"Now to thank you, I'm going to go fix us breakfast," she tells me.

We decide to bring our breakfast back down to Mollie's basement and, as we eat, I point to the area by the bathroom. "Right where the washer and dryer used to be ... wouldn't that be a great place for a small kitchen?"

"Yeah. Maybe I can get Dad to help me with it." Then she points to an open area near her bed. "And the baby's furniture could go right there," she says happily. "Maybe I could get a rocking chair too."

I bite my tongue and nod. "You should be pretty comfortable down here, Mollie. I'm almost starting to feel jealous."

She laughs. "Yeah, right. I'm sure you'd love to trade lives with me."

"Speaking of lives, I should probably get back to my own." I glance up at the French-looking clock that I hung over by the window and stand up to leave.

"But what about practicing for your show?" she asks eagerly. "Don't you want me to coach you?"

"Yes, of course."

"And, don't forget, I still need to pay you back for the stuff you got. Did you save your receipts?"

"I have an idea," I tell her. "Let's just call it an even exchange. You coach me for a while and this will be your payment."

Her eyes grow wide. "You're definitely getting the short end of the stick in that deal."

"Not if you really help me."

"Okay." She nods with a serious expression. "I'll do my best."

So, for the next several hours, with my camera set on the tripod and running, Mollie plays director and I pretend I'm hosting *On the Runway*. We start with me doing a commentary on shabby chic and how it works both in the bedroom and on the catwalk. After this practice episode, we replay what we just filmed and Mollie gives me some fairly blunt but honest critique.

"Pretend the camera is your best friend," she tells me. "You need to relax and smile more."

"That's easier said than done," I point out. "My comfort zone is the *other* side of the camera."

"But how would you like to be filming someone who's treating you like the enemy?"

I consider this. "Good point."

"And quit taking yourself so seriously. Lighten up. Remember that anything can be cut."

"You're really good at this," I tell her. "Do you think you'll continue in film school after the baby comes?"

She sighs. "That's my plan ... but sometimes it feels overwhelming."

Next I do a mock interview with Mollie's old Barbie doll,

which actually turns out to be pretty hilarious. I think it would be fun to try something like this when I do the show about fashion's impact on body image.

We watch this segment, and then Mollie makes me do it again. And then again. By the end of the day, I think I'm either getting better or I'm too tired to know the difference.

As I'm leaving, Mollie thanks me again for her basement makeover and I thank her for coaching me. "We're not done," she reminds me. "But you really made some good progress."

The question is—am I progressing enough to make the cut and help host our show? I'm fully aware that I am not Paige. But as Mollie keeps reminding me, *they don't want me to be Paige*. They want me to be me. But what if me is not good enough?

Chapter
6

Fran schedules the Chanel boutique for our wedding shopping show at the end of the week. Because we shoot it early in the day, before the store opens, Mom is able to come too. But as we're filming, Paige seems a little uneasy about the way that Fran is trying to bring me onto center stage. It's almost like Paige didn't really think we were going to go through with it.

For the sake of the show, we're pretending that Mom hasn't already purchased her wedding clothes. I have a feeling Paige is hoping that she can get Mom to rethink her choice, as she leads her in a completely different direction.

"Look at the soft, flowing lines of this design," Paige tells Mom as she removes a pale peach chiffon number from the rack. "The tea-length skirt would be just perfect in a garden wedding." She holds the dress up in front of Mom, like she's wearing it. But as Mom studies the image in the three-way mirror, her expression is uncertain.

"That doesn't really seem like Mom's style to me," I say as I step next to her.

"And I don't really care for that color," Mom adds.

"Oh, we can see about a different color," Paige insists. "But imagine this dress in a garden wedding. Isn't it sweet and romantic?"

"I don't think I'm really the romantic type." Mom chuckles. "I mean when it comes to fashion."

"I have to agree with Mom," I say. "She's more of a classic."

"Yes." Paige nods. "I'm fully aware of this, but this is for her wedding. What better time to be romantic than at your wedding?"

"But I'm so used to wearing suits and business wear." Mom frowns. "I think I would feel a bit silly in a dress like that."

I pull out a satin two-piece ensemble in a silvery shade of white. "Now I can see you in something like this," I say to Mom as I hold this dress in front of Paige's recommendation. Naturally, Paige tosses me a look—like *why are you showing Mom something that's similar to what she already has?* But I ignore her. "It's sophisticated and classic," I tell Mom. "But this beaded detailing gives it a soft feminine look too."

Mom touches the fabric and smiles. "It's beautiful."

"Why don't you try it on?" the manager suggests.

Mom looks slightly uncomfortable.

"It appears to be your size," the manager tells her.

"Yes, Mom," I urge. "Go try it on while Paige and I look around for bridesmaid dresses."

After Mom goes into the fitting room, Fran suggests that Paige and I split up in the store, each with our own cameraman and doing our own commentary as we look for dresses. JJ follows me, and Alistair trails Paige. Remembering what Mollie said about treating the camera like my best friend, I pretend that JJ is Mollie and just start chatting away.

"I know that Paige wants something softer and lacier," I say quietly to JJ. "Something *romantic*. I realize that would look fabulous on Paige, but Mom and I would probably look silly. And since this is Mom's wedding, I want her to look her best—and to feel comfortable too. You see, my mom and I are really more the classic type. We're just not into frills or lace too much." I finger through the rack, commenting on the various styles and fabrics and colors until I come to one with some good potential.

I pull out the periwinkle satin dress, holding it up for the camera to see. It has cap sleeves and a gently scooped neckline. "See the simple lines, the princess seams … it's a very classic style. Now some people might think that's boring— kind of the way some people think vanilla ice cream is boring. But I happen to love vanilla ice cream. It tastes good with almost anything and it has a timeless appeal. Kind of like this dress." I chuckle. "Of course, most people wouldn't compare dresses to ice cream."

I go over to the three-way mirror again, holding the dress up as if I'm wearing it. "It's really nice. And even though it's a classic, I can imagine it in a garden wedding."

"Would you like to try it on?" the manager asks me.

"Sure." I nod and head over to the fitting room. Paige had us wear the right shoes today so that the dresses we tried on would look better. Before long I have the periwinkle dress on and zipped. It's about a size too big, but close enough to get the picture. When I come out of the fitting room, Mom is dressed in the silver-white suit and standing in front of the mirror with JJ filming her.

"You look beautiful," I tell her as I go and stand beside her. Just then Paige comes back with another saleswoman. Paige is holding a white dress which resembles the earlier one she showed us with a flowing layered skirt, as well as several others in various shades of pink and rose.

"You're already trying dresses on?" she asks me.

"Only this one," I admit.

"I thought you were going to get several," she says as she holds the white gown up for Mom to see. "Now, I know you *think* you want to stick to classic," Paige tells Mom. "But you should at least give this one a try." She smiles brightly. "Just for fun and to make me happy." Then she hands me a rose-colored dress, which again has the soft, layered, romantic look. I have to admit that it's a beautiful dress, but I don't think it'll be beautiful on me.

"What do you think of this one?" Mom asks Paige as she holds out her arms.

"It's nice." Paige nods. "But kind of expected . . . a bit conservative. Plus it's missing any wow appeal."

"Wow appeal?" I echo.

"It's a very safe dress," Paige says with fashion authority. "It would be appropriate for the *mother* of the bride to wear . . . if she wanted to be cautious. But, Mom, you *are* the bride. Don't you want to feel special? Like *wow*."

I can't help but laugh. "What if Mom doesn't want to feel *like wow*?"

Mom laughs. "Okay, Paige, I'll give your dress a try."

"You too," Paige tells me. Then she's literally pushing Mom and me back toward the fitting rooms. I want to protest and ask her why we can't give these other dresses more of a chance, but it's too late. For now that is. As I try on the rose-colored chiffon dress, I decide that I will insist we give the classic styles a second look. Then I get an idea. Maybe we can invite the viewers to vote.

Before long the three of us are standing in front of the mirrors. Naturally, Paige looks stunning, although a bit too princess-like for my taste. But Mom and I both look uncomfortable.

"See," Paige beams. "Isn't this a romantic-looking scene?"

Mom looks like she's trying to be a good sport. "I'll admit the dresses are very pretty, Paige."

"But . . . ?" Paige looks disappointed.

"But this just isn't me." Mom makes a weak smile.

"And it's sure not me," I add. "Although if Mom wanted me to wear this dress, I would do it. Remember, this is Mom's wedding . . . not ours."

"Yes, of course." Paige presses her lips together and nods. "If Mom wants to do classic, then classic it will be. But perhaps we can try some different versions of classic."

So Mom and I cooperate, trying on several more dresses, but we are running out of time and so far I haven't seen anything that everyone can agree on. So, while Paige is out looking again, I decide it's time to step in. "I think we should give the dresses we first tried on another chance," I say to Mom. "The silvery two-piece for you and the periwinkle for me."

Mom smiles. "Yes, let's do that." She turns to the manager. "Perhaps you can find something similar to the periwinkle dress for Paige to try on."

"I know just the one," she tells Mom.

It's not long before Mom and I are standing in front of the mirrors again. "This is more like it," I say.

"I really do like this dress," Mom says as she examines herself in the mirror. She tosses me a glance like maybe she's having second thoughts about the dress she has at home.

"You should get married in the dress you like the most," I assure her.

She smiles. "I love that on you, Erin. It's perfect. I know brides always tell the bridesmaids that they can wear the dresses again, but I actually think you could wear that one again."

I nod. "I think so too."

Paige emerges from the fitting room. Her dress is lilac satin and cut similar to mine, but not exactly the same. Wearing a hard-to-read expression, she joins us. "What do you think, Mom?"

Mom is beaming. "I think it's perfect."

Paige frowns slightly. "Really?"

"What do you think?" Mom asks hopefully.

"Honestly?"

Mom nods. "Yes. You are, after all, the fashion expert, Paige. What do you honestly think?"

"I think it's a bit bland."

Mom looks disappointed. "Oh . . ."

"I disagree," I say. "If we carry the right flowers and—"

"You can't expect flowers to eradicate the blah factor," Paige says.

"I have an idea," I say to the camera. "How about if we let the viewers decide?"

Paige laughs. "You want the viewers to tell our mother what to have for her wedding?"

"I'm not saying that Mom has to make her decision based on the viewers' choice. But it might be fun to hear what they think." I glance over at Fran and she is nodding eagerly. "So . . ." I step closer to the camera. "We want to hear from you. At the end of this show, we'll give you our two best choices and you can let us know what you think."

Fran is signaling to us to wrap it up and I turn to Paige. "Well, this has been fun, hasn't it?"

Paige takes the cue and delivers her traditional line, and then Fran yells cut.

"That was fun," Mom says as we go back to change into our own clothes. "I'll be curious to hear what the viewers think."

"Well, this show won't run for a couple of weeks," Fran tells her. "You might not want to wait that long."

Mom laughs. "No, and that's okay because I've already made up my mind."

Then, to my surprise, Mom actually buys the silvery white satin two-piece dress, as well as the lilac and periwinkle brides-maid dresses for Paige and me. And because we'll be using today's filming on our show, we get a very nice discount. After we leave, Mom tells us that she will return the other dress.

She sighs. "I suppose high fashion is a bit contagious. After wearing that Chanel dress today, I just knew I couldn't be as happy in the other one."

"You're going to look gorgeous," I tell her.

Paige says nothing as we walk back to our cars. But after we part ways, since Mom has to go to work and I'm riding with Paige, my sister opens up.

"I realize that Helen and Fran are encouraging you to take an active role in the show," she says calmly. "But I hope you know what you're doing."

"What do you mean?"

"The reason the show works is because it's about fashion." She says this like she thinks I'm an idiot.

"Yes . . . I know that."

"And the reason that works is because I am the fashion expert."

"Meaning there can be only *one* fashion expert?"

She nods with a confident smile.

"Okay, I realize I'm not an expert," I admit. "But I do have some opinions. And there's more than one kind of fashion. Not everyone is into your expensive forms of haute couture."

"I'm aware of that, Erin." Paige scowls. "What you seem to forget is that real style begins with excellent design. Excellent design translates into haute couture and that does not come cheaply."

"Don't forget that beauty is in the eye of the beholder."

"Don't forget that great designers and haute couture are the foundation of beauty in the fashion arena."

"But what if I happen to think that Granada Ruez is a great designer?"

Paige looks slightly horrified. "Oh, please, Erin. Don't tell me you want to get back on the Granada Greenwear bandwagon."

"Hey, you said you liked her designs after Granada showed you how to wear them."

"I was simply being a good sport. We had a show to do and I wanted to make it a good one."

"Well, Helen wants our show to be broader now," I remind her. "That means more than just high design and haute couture and clothes that only a few can afford."

"You still don't get it, Erin. Good design trickles down from Paris to Wal-Mart. Eventually everyone can afford it. My job is to help them recognize it."

Okay, that actually makes a tiny bit of sense, but I'm not willing to concede just yet.

"I want to help our viewers," she continues. "I care about those fashion-challenged girls who want more style in their lives. What's wrong with giving them what they want?"

"But how do you know what they want? My guess is that our viewers are more like me than you."

She laughs. "See, that's my point. That's why they watch a show like *On the Runway*. They need to be educated about what is and what is not good style."

I groan and lean back. This is so not going to be easy.

"I'm not trying to pick on you, Erin. It's just that the show is working. It's a success and the viewers love it. If we start reinventing it midstream, well, it might hit the rocks and sink."

I consider this. "You could be right."

"I am right."

"So are you saying that Helen Hudson is wrong?"

"No … not exactly. I think she wants to try something different, because that's the way she is, always thinking of new ways to do things. But I'm saying if it's not broken, why fix it?"

"Because it could be even better?"

She firmly shakes her head.

"Well, what about the episode that I was promised about body image and how it's damaged by stick-thin fashion models? Are you suddenly against that?"

"No … not exactly. Because I do feel sorry for girls who think that fashion only comes in one size. That's wrong. But, on the other hand, I wouldn't want us to do too many issue-based shows, like how high heels are bad for feet, or which designers are polluting the planet. It's not as if we're a social documentary program. Or like we think we can fix everyone. I mean, like it or not, we're a show about fashion. We're *On the Runway*, Erin. Not *Dr. Phil*."

I decide it's time to keep my mouth shut about the other show ideas I've been noodling on lately. I should probably run them past Helen and Fran first. And, who knows? Paige could be right. If the show's not broken, maybe it's crazy to attempt to fix it.

Chapter
7

"*I thought you said that Paige and Ben* were history," Mollie says as I drive her home from fellowship group on Saturday night.

I shrug. "Well, that's kind of what she said a couple weeks ago."

Mollie holds up her phone. "I just got a tweet saying the two were spotted at OurHouse this evening."

"At *our* house?" I frown at her. "Huh?"

"OurHouse is a new club in town."

"Oh." I nod.

"Do you think it's serious?"

"I honestly don't know, Mollie." I say this, but I'm starting to feel apprehensive.

"The tweet said they were kissing."

I let out a little groan. "Well … it's her life. Not much I can do about it."

"It could be a publicity stunt."

I cringe. I'm not even sure which is less appealing … that Paige is back with Ben because she really likes him, or that she's back with him for the publicity. And, really, what kind of publicity would that be anyway? I know the old saying that any publicity is good publicity. I just don't happen to agree.

"Although I don't think Paige needs publicity as much as Benjamin does," Mollie continues.

"Seriously?"

"Oh, yeah. Paige is all over the place. You can hardly look at any of the Hollywood gossip sites without seeing Paige's pretty face."

"What kind of gossip is it?"

"The typical stuff—love triangles, secret engagements, fashion tidbits, pictures of Paige around town. Nothing terrible." Mollie laughs. "So you still don't even peek at it?"

"It's just not my thing."

"You've got to be the most reluctant reality TV star out there."

"I'm not a star," I protest.

"Says you."

"Well, I'm not a star like Paige is a star. The truth is I've been rethinking my role as Paige's costar."

"Why would you do that?" Mollie demands. "You were just starting to get good at it. Don't give up before you even begin."

"It's not that I'm giving up, exactly."

"What do you mean?"

"I'm only questioning whether it makes sense or not."

"Why wouldn't it make sense?"

"It's like Paige keeps saying—the show is a success as it is. Why change it?"

Mollie doesn't respond and I hope she's getting it.

"And even though Paige and I have our differences ... she's my sister and I love her. I don't want to ruin a show that's already working. You know?"

"Yeah, that makes sense."

"Anyway, I have a meeting with Helen and Fran this Monday. I'm supposed to run my ideas past them ... and we'll see."

"I'm sure they'll do what's best for the show, Erin. It's not like they'll want to mess it up."

"I know."

I'll admit I'm disappointed that I might not get to do the shows I've been planning. But at the same time it might be a relief to be free from all the pressures. Maybe there'll be another way to share my opinions about style and fashion.

But at the meeting on Monday, to my surprise both Fran and Helen seem totally open to my ideas.

"The key to good reality TV is to be open to shaking it up a bit," Fran tells me.

"Shake it but don't break it," Helen adds.

"So we'll play with some controversies," Fran tells Helen. "If they don't work, we can always cut them later." Then she explains her plan to us. "As you know, Paige will continue in the lead, but we'll introduce a seven-minute segment that I'm calling 'Sibling Rivalry' where the girls will go head-to-head over fashion." Fran turns to me. "You'll gather your facts as well as some footage of interviews or fashion shows or whatever you can use to back up your opinions. We'll let you both have at it, then do some editing and see how it works."

"Excellent!" Helen claps her hands together. "I can just imagine."

"Seven minutes isn't much time," I point out. "I thought

that I was going to get a whole show to focus on body image and fashion." I hold up the proposal sheet I put together for "Killer Style: What Happens When Fashion Turns Lethal?"

Helen frowns. "I know you wanted to do that show, Erin. But the more I thought about using an entire *On the Runway* episode to cover this issue, the more concerned I got. Fans expect the show to be upbeat and fun. We need to maintain that general feeling."

"Upbeat and fun with a little edge," Fran says. "Just like the 'Sibling Rivalry' segment will add."

"We want you to take the lead in deciding what the controversial topics can be, Erin. But we can't let the show become too negative. Do you get that?" Helen studies me.

"I get it," I tell them. "And I guess I'm not that surprised."

"Who knows ..." Helen gives me a sly smile. "Maybe the 'Sibling Rivalry' segment will catch on and you'll have your own spin-off show."

"It happens." Fran looks down at what appears to be a schedule. "The plan is to film some of these segments before we go to London. We'll insert them into some shows and see how viewers respond."

"In the meantime," Helen tells me, "we still expect you to act as Paige's costar during the other filming. Be yourself."

"That's right," Fran tells me. "Feel free to mix it up like you did at Chanel last week."

Helen nods. "I saw outtakes this morning. It looked good. So keep it up, Erin. Express yourself and your opinions."

"I'll go over these ideas," Fran tells me as she puts my stack of possible show topics into a folder, "and see what we can line up to shoot between now and London. We have only ten days before we have to leave."

As we exit the room, I think about what Fran and Helen proposed. It's not exactly what I had imagined, but I'm open to it. And maybe I'm actually relieved ... some of the pressure is off. I'm sure Paige will be happy too. She'll probably love the idea of arguing fashion with me. Not that she's been talking to me much lately. I'm not sure if it's because she thinks I'm infringing on her fame or if she's simply feeling guilty for "secretly" dating Benjamin again. Whatever it is, I decide it's time to find out. Now if I can only think of a non-confrontational way to bring it up.

Paige is watching TV when I come into the house. But when I see she's watching *Britain's Got Style*, I realize this is about work, not entertainment. "Doing research?" I ask.

She nods as she takes a drink of iced tea. "Fran sent these DVDs over last week."

I want to ask why no one told me about this, but I realize that might ignite a feud. Instead, I sit down and watch with her. The main host of this show, Chloe Brinkman, used to be in a music group and then did some modeling, but now she's best known as Brit's number-one fashion diva. And she's very opinionated. However, I find that I agree with much of her take on fashion and modeling. In fact, by the time the show ends, I find I rather like Chloe Brinkman.

"She's really good," I say as I get a glass of iced tea for myself.

"Who?" Paige calls.

"Chloe Brinkman." I return to see Paige slipping in another DVD.

"Oh ... she's okay."

"Just okay?" I sit down and wait.

"She's not as much of an expert as she wants everyone to

think." Paige points the remote at the TV and the next DVD starts playing.

I'm tempted to argue this "fact," but decide to save it for one of our "Sibling Rivalry" segments. "I met with Fran and Helen this morning," I say offhandedly.

"How'd that go?" She turns the volume down slightly.

I study her for a few seconds. I can tell by her expression that this isn't a surprise to her. "Okay."

"So they told you about the 'Sibling Rivalry' thing they want to do?"

"You knew about it?"

She pauses the DVD then turns and blinks at me. "Of course I knew about it. Did you think they would've told you before they told me?"

"Well ... no ... not really." Okay, I actually did think this. Not that I plan to admit it.

"I told them I think it'll flop, but it's worth a try."

"Right ..."

"Did Fran tell you that we're set to shoot more film for our bridal episode?"

"I thought we were done with it."

"No. We need to fill out the show with a few more designers."

"But Mom already made up—"

"This isn't about Mom, Erin." She lets out an exasperated sigh. "It's about our show."

"Oh ... okay." I try to sound positive. "So what do we do? Pretend to still be shopping for bridesmaid dresses?"

She nods. "That's the general plan. First we'll look at the Vera Wang collection and then we'll head over to check out a new designer—a guy who used to design for Badgley

Mischka and is trying to set up a studio in LA. Fran just heard about him."

"Fran said we'll shoot some 'Sibling Rivalry' segments this week too."

"That should be fun." Paige makes a face.

"Are you okay with it?" I ask a bit tentatively.

She smiles, but it looks slightly forced. "Yeah, sure. I think it'll be fun."

"Also, just so you know, I've been thinking about what you were saying the other day—about how the show already works, and how we don't want to mess that up."

"And?"

"And I think you're mostly right."

She looks relieved.

"I mean, I can still have my opinions," I add quickly. "We don't have to agree on everything."

"That's what Helen and Fran are hoping for."

"So we should be okay ... right?"

She nods. "Yes. I'm sorry if I bit your head off the other day. I think I was kind of stressed."

"Speaking of stressed ... Mollie mentioned that you and Benjamin have been a topic on Twitter and some of the Holly-wood gossip shows."

Paige just smiles.

"So are you guys dating?"

Her smile fades. "No, of course not. Remember, I told you that I gave that all up."

"But you're seeing him?"

She nods with a catty smile. "And the media is eating it up."

"You're only doing it for publicity?"

"It's a win-win for everyone, Erin."

I frown at her. "How is that even possible?"

"Benjamin needs publicity right now ... and a little more face-in-the-news time doesn't hurt us either."

"But hasn't Ben kind of been *bad* news lately? I mean, the whole thing with Mia was only a couple of months ago. I don't see how you being photographed with him can help our show much."

"You'd be surprised, Erin. Plus it's ratings sweeps next month. We need to keep this thing rolling." She gives me a perturbed look. "It's not like you're doing anything to help in that regard."

I'm not sure how to react to that one.

"But that's okay," she says in a slightly patronizing tone. "We don't expect you to get out there and get your hands dirty."

"What's that supposed to mean?"

"You know what it means." Paige gives me her devious grin. "You're the good sister ... and I'm the wild one."

"I thought we were *both* good sisters."

She nods. "We are. But I have an image to maintain. I have fans to amuse."

"I so don't get that."

"I know." She clicks the remote, causing the DVD to play again. "I didn't expect that you would."

I watch the show for a while, but I find myself getting more and more aggravated at my sister. It gets to the point where I can't even focus on Chloe Brinkman anymore. And yet, when I sneak a glance at Paige, she's calmly watching, like she's totally oblivious to what she just said or how it might have sounded. Then I wonder if I'm overreacting. Finally, I get up and leave. But once I'm in my room, I call Mollie and tell her what happened. "It's like Paige doesn't care what people think of her," I say finally. "Like it's no big deal that she's going to clubs with a guy who came very close to being prosecuted for manslaughter, and still hasn't stopped drinking. I mean, he could be behind bars right now. Instead, he's running around with my sister, making the front pages of the gossip rags."

Mollie simply laughs. "And that's called publicity."

"If I hear that word again—I think I'll scream."

"It's what sells things like reality TV shows, Erin. Surely you know that by now."

"I know it," I seethe. "I just don't like it."

"Then you are in the wrong business."

I consider this. "Yeah, you're right. I probably am."

"Okay ... sorry not to sound more sympathetic," she says. "But I'm sitting here feeling the world is passing me by and you're complaining about publicity. Man, I'd love to have your problems, Erin."

"Sorry." I shake my head and wonder why I'm apologizing to her.

"Hey, in happier news, my parents got home last night and couldn't believe what you did to the basement."

"They were okay with it?"

"Yeah. They were almost *too* okay with it. Suddenly my mom was rethinking her plan to take over my old bedroom. Like she might rather set up her writing studio in the basement now."

"No way. That's *your* basement."

Mollie laughs, but I can hear a trace of sadness mixed in. "Yeah, that's what I told them. It's my basement ... for now anyway."

We talk awhile longer and I begin to feel guilty for complaining about Paige and her recent publicity stunts. Really, it's a small thing compared to what Mollie is dealing with right now. After we hang up, I think about Tony's role in all this, and how he was so into Mollie—until she got pregnant, that is. Now he's pulled this amazing and mysterious disappearing act. I'd almost like to hunt him down and give him a piece of my mind, not that he would listen. In fact, I'm starting to suspect that no one wants to listen to any of my strong opinions.

Chapter
8

"So are you girls okay with these?" Marty
Stuart asks as he hands us the revised contracts that he's been
negotiating with Helen Hudson.

"I am," I tell him as I pick up a pen and get ready to sign.

"I'm not." Paige pushes her contract back across his desk.

"Huh?" I study her expression. "What's wrong? You want
more money?" I actually thought the pay increase was pretty
generous.

"No, it's not about the money."

"What is it then?" Marty looks perplexed too.

"I don't like the 'Sibling Rivalry' idea. I think it will only
slow down the show and bore the viewers. Besides that, I
want creative sign-off on the show. And I want the assurance
that I will continue as the host — the *only* host. And I want it
in writing."

Too stunned to respond, I just stare at my sister, curious
as to whether I can actually see her head increasing in size.
What is going on with her? And what's up with this prima
donna act? She can't be serious.

Marty looks slightly nervous. "The *only* host?"

"Yes. I don't want to share that spot with anyone."

"Not even Erin?" He glances back and forth between us.

"I'm happy to see Erin moving beyond Camera Girl in the show," she says carefully. "I'm fine with that. But I do not want the 'Sibling Rivalry' segment and I do not want to share my host position with anyone. Not even my sister." She turns and smiles sweetly at me. "Surely you understand that, don't you?"

I nod slowly, trying to think of a way out of this mess. "I do … understand." And this is true; in a strange and slightly twisted way I do understand. And in a way, I'm not completely blindsided by this either. Hurt, yes; surprised, not so much. I mean, this is Paige. "But what about Helen?" I ask carefully.

"Oh, I think Helen will understand too."

"Meaning what?" Now I realize my sister is full of herself, but I can't believe she thinks she can overstep Helen. I mean, how can she be so nonchalant? She's about to tell Helen that she plans to take over the show, and it's like she honestly thinks Helen is going to just say "no problem."

"Don't worry, Erin. Helen will get this."

"But what if she doesn't? What happens then?"

Paige presses her lips together.

"Erin poses a good question," Marty tells Paige. "What if Helen *doesn't* agree?"

Paige shrugs. "In that case, maybe I'll just walk."

"Walk?" I stare at Paige, wondering who this girl is and what she's done with my sister. "You must be kidding. You love this show."

She sighs. "I *used* to love the show."

"So what are you saying then?" Marty asks. "You're done with it? After a few months?"

"I'm simply saying *On the Runway* isn't the only show in town."

"Seriously? You think you can get another show as good as this?" I shake my head doubtfully.

"Maybe even better."

Marty grabs a pencil and starts jotting on a notepad. "So you're sure this is what you want, Paige? You really want to make a demand like this to Helen?"

"I do."

"*Paige?*" I want to shake her. Like *wake up*—why is she nuking her show and her career like this? At the same time, I think why not let her—get it over with. It's bound to happen; the sooner the better.

"What, Erin?" She looks evenly at me.

"What if you do this and it blows up in your face? Are you seriously going to go looking for another show after less than six months on this one?"

"Erin has a point." Marty continues writing. "You haven't even done a full season on your show. The industry won't take that sort of thing lightly."

Paige holds her head high. "I'm not worried."

"How can you not be worried?" I ask. "I'm worried and this show isn't as big a deal to me as I know it is to you. How can you be so calm about this?"

"Because I know I will land on my feet."

A little light goes on in my brain. "So ... who have you been talking to?"

"No one." But her eyes betray her. I can tell she's been talking to someone. And I have a pretty good idea who.

"*Benjamin Kross.*" I pound my fist on the desk. "What's he been telling you, Paige? That you're a big star now? That you can get more money somewhere else? That you should pull the prima donna act and make your demands, stomp your designer shoe and get your way?"

She shrugs.

"Is Benjamin offering you something specific?" Marty persists. "A new reality show perhaps?"

"Let's say this . . . I have my opportunities."

"So, just for clarification's sake," I say, "if Helen *doesn't* agree . . . that means you really plan to walk away from the show? Is that right?"

"I can't predict the future, Erin. I don't know which way this will go. I honestly don't expect Helen to balk at this."

"But you would walk if she did? You would, wouldn't you?" I can't believe she's so cool about this.

"Probably."

I'm so frustrated I feel close to tears. "Do you know how selfish that is, Paige?"

"Selfish to look after my own future?" She looks honestly confused, like the idea of selfishness never even occurred to her. "If I don't take care of my career, who will? Don't forget that I'm the one who wanted to do this in the first place. You know that you've been reluctant from the get-go, Erin."

"I may have been reluctant, but I did give up film school to do this show with you, Paige! I put my life on hold and dropped everything just to—"

"And look at the experience you've gotten from it!" she shouts back. "Do you honestly think you'd have learned this much in school?"

"Time out!" Marty says loudly. "Both of you take a big deep breath and chill for a minute. Okay?"

His office grows quiet and all I hear is the scratching of

his pencil on paper as he continues to write notes. Then he punches his phone and calls in his assistant, tapping his pencil on the desk as he waits for her to come. When she arrives, he hands her Paige's contract along with his notes, and asks her to make the revisions and new copies. After she leaves he folds his hands on the desk in front of him and shakes his head. "I can't say that I approve of this decision, Paige, but I do understand. And as your agent, I am willing to do my best to get Helen Hudson to agree to this."

"Thank you." Paige reaches for her bag.

Marty looks directly at me now. "It would probably help if you agreed to it as well, Erin."

"In writing?"

He smiles. "I mean more of in spirit . . ."

I shrug. It's weird, but I think I'm relieved. Maybe this crazy ride is about to end. Maybe I can part ways with Paige without feeling guilty now. Maybe I can have my life back. And yet it hurts. "I guess I can agree. I mean, it's not like I have much of a choice." I hold up my contract. "Do you still want me to sign this?"

"If you're still okay with it. Paige's revisions don't really impact your contract."

"Well, other than the fact that it might make my contract worthless."

"I'm not doing this to hurt you," Paige says in a flat tone.

"Yeah . . . right." I don't even look at her as I sign my name and the date.

"But you're still mad at me, aren't you?"

I take in another deep breath, trying to hold back tears as I open another copy, looking for the right line to sign on. I'm not even sure why this hurts so much. Other than the fact it feels like my sister just knifed me in the back. But, really, I should be relieved. Maybe this will end this insane sister act once and for all. Because, honestly, I don't think I can take anymore of this. With a tightened jaw and imagining that I am signing divorce papers—to divorce my sister—I sign the last copy and slide it all back over to Marty.

"If my work here is done, I'd like to go," I tell him as I stand. Thankfully, Paige and I took separate cars here today. I'm ready to make a quick exit.

He nods. "Thanks, Erin."

"Thank you," I say with a lump in my throat.

With a sad expression, Marty stands and reaches out to shake my hand. For some reason it feels like a farewell gesture. Like he's telling me this is it—time to kiss *On the Runway* adios. Then, without saying a word to my sister, I leave.

I get in my Jeep and just sit there. Really, I don't know why I'm taking this so hard. Paige is right ... the show was never my dream in the first place. I've been dragging my heels since day one. And, while it hurts a little to see everything just vanish, that's not the most disturbing part of this.

The hardest thing is feeling like my own sister has dismissed me. Like she's been using me all along and now she's done and ready to move on ... like see ya later, little sister.

I remember other times like this. Not as hurtful perhaps, but painfully similar. Paige always had a hard time getting and maintaining friends. Of course, I have my own suspicions as to why this happens. I still recall a number of times when Paige, between friends, would solicit me as her "little buddy." I'd usually try to accommodate her. Of course, this usually meant getting stuck in some inane activity like playing Barbies or dress-up, or sneaking into Mom's makeup and taking the blame once we were found out.

What I remember today is how Paige and I would be in the middle of some crazy Paige-directed activity and I'd be trying to "cooperate" (which meant doing things her way), and out of the blue one of her friends would call and invite her to do something. And—just like that—Paige would dump me like last year's bell bottoms.

I feel just as horrible now. Since I don't want to go home, because Paige will probably end up there too, I drive over to Mollie's. But she's at a doctor's appointment.

"She should be back in about half an hour," Mrs. Tyson tells me. "At least she better be back since she borrowed my car and I have a meeting to go to at two."

"Oh." I step back. "Okay."

"But you can wait for her if you like."

Normally I wouldn't care to do this, but right now I'd like someplace to just lie low. "Okay," I agree. "I guess I'll do that."

"I'm sure you can find the way to her new room," Mrs. Tyson says in a way that's hard to decipher.

"Right." I glance at her. "Was the makeover okay?"

"Oh, sure." She folds her arms across her front. "We'd been encouraging her to move down there. And it looks very nice. But . . ."

"But?" I pause and look directly at her.

"But Mollie's father and I were hoping she'd fix up the room herself, Erin. We didn't want anyone to help her."

"You didn't want anyone to help her?"

She shakes her head.

"Why not?"

"Well, as her father says, she got herself into this mess and she should have to get herself out of it."

I frown at her and it takes all my self-control not to say something totally regrettable. I guess I should've known better. Mollie warned me that her dad was not taking her pregnancy well. It seems clear he has influenced her mom now too. "I'm sorry if helping Mollie offended you," I say in a stiff voice. "But it seemed like she needed some help."

Mrs. Tyson makes a look like *duh*, but says nothing.

"I know you guys are Christians." I push this a bit further. "And Jesus tells us to treat others how we want to be treated . . . so I guess that's what I was trying to do."

"Yes. I suppose that makes sense . . . to you."

"But not to you?"

"You know I love Mollie, Erin." She frowns. "But I have to agree with her father on this. If Mollie doesn't step up and own her problems—in this case a child—well, then she'll never grow up . . . will she?"

"I think she's growing up."

She chuckles. "Well, I suppose we're both just looking at Mollie from two different places now, aren't we?"

"I guess so." I can't help but get the implication here that I, like Mollie, am young and have a lot to learn still. And maybe it's true. But maybe parents forget that it takes time to get this stuff. Maybe they don't remember how things were when they were younger. Or maybe growing up just came easier to them.

"But I'm glad that Mollie has some good mature friends like you," Mrs. Tyson says as I open the door to the stairway.

I force a smile. "Oh, I'm not sure that I'm all that mature," I say lightly. "Just a few minutes ago I wanted to take a swing at my sister. That's not terribly grown up."

She looks slightly horrified. "You wanted to hit that beautiful sister of yours?"

I nod. "Yeah … actually I did."

"Oh, Erin. She's been so good to let you be on her TV show. I would think you'd be more grateful."

"I guess we're both just looking at Paige from two different places," I say to her.

She frowns and then smiles in a slightly condescending way. "Well, I'm sure you and Paige will work it out."

"Yes. I'm sure we will." Then I go downstairs, pick up one of the pillows that Mollie and I re-covered a few days ago, and soundly punch it.

When Mollie gets home, we commiserate over our problems together. I can tell it's a consolation to Mollie to hear that all is not smooth sailing with Paige and the show. But she has the sense not to say that.

"You know Paige will come around," Mollie says with confidence. "If Helen doesn't agree to her demands, Paige will cave. She loves that show, Erin. She's not about to let it go. You know that old saying, 'A bird in the hand is worth two in the bush.'"

"But what if Paige's other birds aren't in the bush?" I protest. "What if she's got one bird in the right hand and two in the left?"

Mollie laughs. "I guess that wouldn't surprise me."

"I'll bet Benjamin has something brewing," I speculate. "Something he wants Paige to be involved in so that it will help his ratings."

Mollie opens her laptop. "How about if I check out the gossip sites and see if I can find something?"

I sink down onto her re-covered sofa and sigh. "I'm not sure I even want to know. Or that I even care."

"Don't forget that knowledge is power, Erin. You shouldn't keep your head in the sand as much as you do."

"Really, I should be happy that this crazy ride is over," I say, mostly to myself since Mollie seems absorbed by the computer now. "I mean, now I can go back to school." I shake my head. "Although it'll be like starting over again. Everyone else will be ahead of me now."

"Hey, here's something about Benjamin Kross talking to someone at Bravo."

"Bravo? What's that?"

"Man, Erin, you really do live under a rock, don't you?"

"Okay ... I remember now. It's the high-end reality TV channel."

"Something like that."

"So what does it say specifically?"

"Not much. There's also something about his movie deal ... like it's still a possibility. Especially after last week's episode of *Malibu Beach*. Did you see that?"

I groan. "No, thanks, I'm not really into that."

"Well, it was actually pretty good. I mean it seemed genuine and heartfelt. Benjamin even cried."

"Good for Benjamin."

Mollie looks up from her computer now. "Sometimes it sounds like you hate him, Erin."

I press my lips together and try to examine my feelings.

"Do you hate him?"

"I don't know exactly. I hope that I don't hate him. I mean, it's wrong to hate anyone, no matter how twisted they are."

"Yeah." She nods soberly. "And, trust me, I know how that feels whenever I think about Tony."

I consider this. "That has to be a lot harder," I admit. "It's so much more personal. When I think about you and Tony, I even feel like I hate him."

"You need to get over this, Erin. Hate isn't good for you."

I smile at the irony. "Seems like I was just telling you that."

"I know. But my obstetrician told me that my blood pressure seemed a little high today."

"Your blood pressure?"

Mollie nods. "She said I need to keep things calm."

"Did you tell your mom about this yet?" I'm recalling her parents' attitude about how Mollie needs to grow up and take responsibility for things.

"No . . ."

"You better let her know, Mollie."

She looks back at her computer screen. "Here's another juicy piece about Benjamin and your sister."

I groan. "I'm not sure I want to hear it."

"It says here that they were rumored to have had a secret rendezvous in Paris."

"I can only imagine who leaked that one. It's not like the paparazzi were trailing us."

"You think Ben leaked it?"

"Use your imagination."

"So what if he and Paige really did get serious?" Mollie asks me.

I shrug. "Not much I can do about that."

"Besides lose the attitude?"

"Hey, I'm working on it."

She laughs and closes her computer. "Yeah, I can tell."

I lean back and sigh. "Do you remember when life was simple?"

"Was it ever simple?"

I frown to think about how my life feels slightly out of control lately … How my mom's getting married and moving out to live with Jon. How my sister seems intent on blowing up our show and going in her own direction, which might include a guy I don't respect. Plus, I've only got one term of college under my belt when most other kids my age are finishing their first year.

"You know, like back when we were kids," I tell her. "Do you think we'll ever get to live like that again?"

"I think we had our chance," she says glumly.

"Too bad we didn't appreciate it more, huh?"

She shakes her head as she rubs her rounded stomach. "Yeah. Like they say, you don't know what you got until it's gone."

I guess that's pretty much true. The sad part is I can remember being so eager to grow up—like I couldn't get there fast enough. Now I'm suddenly old enough to supposedly manage my own life, and all I want is to go back and be a kid again. It just figures.

Chapter
9

My cell phone rings just as I'm leaving Mollie's house, and my caller ID informs me it's Helen Hudson. I get inside my Jeep to answer, trying not to sound too nervous. "Hi, Helen."

"Erin." Her deep voice has a chilly calmness to it. Almost like the hush before the hurricane. "What is going on with your sister?"

"What do you mean?"

"I mean I've got a revised contract here with Paige's name on it and I want to know *what's going on*."

"Maybe you should ask Paige about—"

"Have no doubts, I definitely plan to speak to Paige, but I wanted to hear your thoughts first."

"Oh."

"I'm curious as to how you feel about big sister trying to shove you back into the corner."

I take in a deep breath and carefully consider my answer. Maybe it was talking to Mollie ... or maybe it was just taking time to chill, but I no longer feel so enraged at my sister. "I don't think Paige is actually trying to shove me back into the corner."

"You don't?"

"No ... not exactly."

"Well, maybe you didn't see this revised contract."

"I have a pretty good idea of what's in it."

"And you're okay with that? No 'Sibling Rivalry' segment. Paige has creative control. You are relegated to ... well, pretty much to where you've been before."

"I know that Paige has a need to be in the spotlight," I say slowly. "I'm used to this."

"Yes, yes ... I know you don't mind playing second fiddle, Erin. But I think your sister wants to be the *only* fiddle—in fact, she seems to believe she's the entire orchestra."

"I don't disagree ... but isn't that why you hired Paige in the first place?"

"Producing a successful reality TV show requires more than one star, Erin."

"But hasn't the show *been* successful?"

"Yes, but this is the result of a team effort. I assumed that you, more than most, might understand this, Erin. After all, you were going to film school. Don't they teach that sort of thing anymore?"

I consider reminding her that I barely even started film school, but have a feeling it wouldn't do much good. Besides, she's right. Good production is the result of a good team. "If it's any consolation, I was pretty mad at Paige to start with," I say carefully. "I couldn't believe that she wanted to change her contract like that, especially since she told me privately that she was okay with the 'Sibling Rivalry' segment. But at the same time I understand her need to protect her position as the one and only host of the *On the Runway*."

"Even if the producer wants to go in a new direction?"

"I didn't say that I agree with her, Helen. I already warned her that I thought she was taking a risk."

"And?"

"She didn't seem concerned."

"Does she not understand that the way shows like ours remain hot and viable is that they are able to shift gears and change directions quickly—reality TV is like a living, breathing art form. It needs room to grow and adapt—to be able to catch the next wave. I feel that Paige's new contract will cut us off from that kind of flexibility. *On the Runway* will become stale and stagnant."

"Not as stale and stagnant as it would become without her," I counter.

"Touché. Your loyalty to your backstabbing sister is moving."

I force a small laugh. "Thanks."

"Erin, be straight with me. Is someone offering Paige another show? Is your sister looking for greener pastures? Because if she is, she's not only incredibly naïve, but she is going to be in a mountain of trouble too. I'll have my attorneys on this so fast that Paige's pretty little head will look like she should be starring in *The Exorcist*."

I honestly don't know how to respond to this. Part of me wants to protect and defend my sister, but another part gets Helen's anger. I don't say anything.

"I have two questions for you, Erin."

"Yes?"

"One, do you think Paige is trying to leave the show? And, two, do you feel ready to step up and take her place?"

"Wow ... I don't know."

"You don't know the answer to *either* question?"

"I honestly don't, Helen. As far as Paige goes, she's not exactly communicating with me and I'm not a psychic. You'll have to talk to her. As for me hosting the show ... well, the truth is that's flattering, but totally overwhelming."

"Yes. I expected you'd say something like that, but I appreciate your honesty. Now one more question."

"What?"

"Will you be terribly disappointed if we go back to the original format for the show—with Paige acting as the one and only host, the diva of divine style, the goddess of good taste, the final say in fashion?" She laughs in a sarcastic tone, although I suspect she knows that's not much of an exaggeration since the media sources have been saying pretty much the same thing.

"Not at all. It's your show, Helen."

"Really? You're not just a little disappointed to be shoved back into the corner away from the limelight?"

"I still wish we could address some of those tough topics that concern me, like how anorexic models impact the rest of us. But maybe Paige is right. Maybe that belongs on a different show."

"I have an idea, Erin."

"What's that?"

"Another avenue you might take. Tell me ... are you a good writer?"

"I guess I'm okay."

"Why don't you start a blog or something on the Internet to get your opinions and information across?"

"A blog?"

"Or a website or some other kind of media access."

"Do you honestly think anyone would read it?"

"You don't seem to appreciate that you have a platform now, Erin. Because of your role, albeit small, on a hot reality show like *On the Runway*, people are interested in you. They want to hear what you think. If your selfish sister won't let you get your opinions onto the show, you can always get them out through other means." Helen laughs. "I know you believe in God, Erin. Haven't you heard that saying—when God closes a door, he opens a window. Remember the line from *The Sound of Music*?"

As I'm chewing on this, Helen says she has to take a call. "Now don't tell Paige we talked," she says quickly. "And don't mention this to Fran either. I'd just as soon keep Fran removed from the sticky negotiation side of things. Don't want to sour her against our Princess Paige." She laughs, but I can tell she still doesn't think this is too funny. Then she says good-bye.

By the time I get home, Paige is pacing in the kitchen like a nervous cat. I can tell by the twist of her mouth she's starting to get worried. I know I could try to console her a bit, but I decide to just let her brew for a while. Without saying a word, I head straight to my room, but I've barely closed the door when my phone rings and I'm surprised to see it's Blake. I think this is the first time he's called me since I told him I wanted to cool it after the Paris trip.

"Hey, Blake," I say in a friendly tone. "What's up?"

"That's what I'm wondering . . . *what is up?*"

"Huh?"

"Well, I was just with Benjamin and it sounds like he and Paige have been going out . . . and I thought you said that you and your sister made some kind of sisterly agreement to have a non-dating pact so that you could focus on your show without the distraction of guys." His tone sounds frosty.

"Yeah ... well, that agreement has been steadily deteriorating." I quickly explain how Paige seems to have cheated on me. "But, trust me, that's only the tip of the iceberg right now."

"What do you mean?"

"Oh, it's just some messed-up stuff in regard to our show. I probably shouldn't even say anything."

"Unless you need to talk. Because you sound frustrated, Erin. You know me — I don't always have answers, but I think I'm a pretty good listener."

It's so good to hear Blake's voice again. So I just open the gates and the whole story spills out about the revised contract and Helen's reaction and how Paige might want to be on a different show. "But please don't tell anyone."

"You know you can trust me."

I think I can trust him ... I *believe* I can trust him. Yet he did break my heart once. Although, to be fair, that was a year ago and for the past six months he's been rock solid. Still ... I should probably keep my guard up. "Most of all, please, don't mention it to Benjamin," I say finally. "The last thing we need is for him to know more about what's going on than Paige."

"You have my word, Erin."

"Thanks ... and thanks for listening."

"So, tell me ... what's the deal now? On dating, I mean."

"For me?"

"Yeah. I don't want to pressure you, and I'm willing to go back to the just friends thing as long as I know that I'm still on your short list — hopefully a really short list — of guys you might potentially go out with."

I think about this. "Well, absolutely, I want you as my friend, Blake. I've missed going out with you. But regardless of how Paige handles her love life or keeps her promises, I still kind of feel that I'm not ready to get seriously involved—and I mean with anyone."

"But if you were?"

I laugh. "Well, of course, you'd be on my very short, short list, Blake. Don't you know that?"

He laughs too. "I had hoped that was the case ... but sometimes I feel a little insecure. It's not easy being infatuated with a star."

"A star?" I laugh even louder now. "Did you suffer a recent head injury? Because it sounds like maybe you're seeing stars."

"Hey, I'm serious, Erin. You don't seem to get that your popularity has steadily increased since the makeover segment in Paris. Don't you ever pay attention to this stuff?"

"If you mean tweets or social networks or tabloids or the polls or the gossip shows, I honestly *don't* pay attention. In fact, I get most of my information from Mollie—usually whether I want to hear it or not."

"See ... and that's just one more thing I like about you. This stuff never seems to go to your head. So back to whether or not you'll go out with me—and I don't mean so that we can get seriously involved—I get that. But, how about it—do you want to go grab a burger or something with me tonight?"

"That actually sounds good." The truth is, I wasn't looking forward to being stuck at home with my mixed-up sister this evening. After we set a time and hang up, I get ready to go, waiting in my room until I hear the doorbell. Paige is still pacing in the kitchen as I hurry to answer the door.

"I'm going out with Blake," I call to her, not waiting for a response, then I slip out and close the door.

"I'm starting to feel a little bit sorry for her," I admit as Blake drives away from the condo.

"Why?"

"I don't know ... but sometimes it feels like Paige is her own worst enemy."

He nods like he gets this. "Maybe it's because she almost always gets what she wants."

I think about this. "You know, you could be right. She does almost always get what she wants. But sometimes it turns out that what she wants isn't necessarily the best thing for her."

"That's why it's kind of cool to turn things over to God ... to wait when he says wait, or to trust that him saying no might turn out to be a good thing."

I study Blake as he drives, and it might just be me, but I think this boy is growing up.

"I thought we'd made an agreement," Paige says to me as soon as I come into the house.

"Huh?" I set my bag on the table by the door and study her. She's wearing warm-ups and her face, devoid of makeup, harbors an expression that reminds me of our childhood. Not exactly pouting, but slightly hurt.

"We agreed we weren't going to date."

"Oh, that." I wave my hand. "Rumor has it you already broke that agreement. And now I'm following your fine example."

Her eyebrows shoot up. "What do you mean?"

I shake my head. "Seriously, Paige, you follow that stuff. You know exactly what I mean."

"Do you mean Benjamin?"

I give her my best *duh* look and wait for her to explain.

"Well, that's nothing."

"Nothing?" I stare at her, wondering if she honestly expects me to swallow that.

"Of course it's nothing, Erin. Surely you knew that."

"How would I possibly know that?" I kick off my shoes. "It's not like you talk to me."

"I talk to you," she says indignantly.

"Right. You tell me one thing and then you do the opposite. That's a great way to communicate."

"What do you mean?"

"Are you serious?" I stare at her. "You know what you've done, Paige. Don't act like you don't."

"You mean by protecting my career?"

"By throwing your sister under the bus?"

"I never did that."

"Right." I shake my head. "And I'll never write a book called *Sister Dearest* either."

"Huh?" She looks honestly clueless and this makes me want to just shake her.

"Where's Mom?" I ask as I go into the kitchen to escape her.

"With Jon." She follows me. "Besides, you're the one who doesn't talk to me, Erin. I know you've been avoiding me."

"I'm talking to you now." I fill a glass with water.

"So, tell me then, why is it okay for you to go out with Blake?"

I am determined to remain calm as I look evenly at her. "Why is it okay for you to go out with Ben?"

"You honestly don't know the answer to that? You don't know why I go out with Benjamin Kross? Are you really that dumb?"

I give her a blank look.

"It's about *publicity*, little sister. Haven't you noticed how much I've been in the spotlight this past week?" Her eyes twinkle and I can tell how much she loves this—being the center of attention. It makes my stomach hurt.

"You seriously think Ben is good publicity?"

"You know what they say about publicity, Erin."

"But you're already in the spotlight," I try to reason. "You have that without Ben. You don't need him."

"You really don't get it, do you?"

I frown. "No, apparently not."

"It's like this ball is rolling, Erin. But I need to help keep it rolling. It won't just roll by itself."

I set my empty glass in the sink. "Really?"

She firmly shakes her head. Judging by her expression, she believes herself. "No. It's up to me to keep it going. And that means getting attention when and how I can."

"So you're saying that you and Benjamin aren't really dating?"

"Not in the romantic sense."

"Says you."

Paige takes a small bunch of grapes from the fridge and pops one into her mouth.

"But you can't speak for Ben, can you?" I persist. "What if he's serious?"

"Oh, Erin, you know it takes two to tango." She laughs and pops another grape into her mouth.

"Well, just so you know, I told Blake that I'm not going to

get seriously involved with him or anyone for a while. And I plan to stick to my guns. But I don't think it'll hurt to go out with him occasionally." I flash her a snide smile. "You know, for publicity."

She rolls her eyes. "Whatever."

"Not that we'll need much of that if our show shuts down."

"Our show is not shutting down, Erin."

"What makes you so sure?"

"Because I just got off the phone with Helen Hudson."

"Oh …?"

"Don't act so innocent. I know she already talked to you."

"So."

"So we've reached an agreement."

"Which is?"

"Which is I will be the sole host and star of the show, but you will be my supporting costar."

"Supporting costar as in playing Camera Girl?" Although I should be relieved to go back to this role, I'm still mad.

She seems to study me, like she's taking some kind of inventory or maybe even about to critique my outfit, which is more my style than hers. I'm ready to defend myself.

"No … I mean supporting costar as in playing yourself and my little sister. If you feel the need to lug your camera around, well, it's okay with me. Although Helen might disagree. But I will draw the line at you trying to upstage me. Either I remain the star of *On the Runway* or I will walk."

I give her a blasé look. "And that's supposed to surprise me?"

"I wasn't trying to surprise you … I was simply trying to make myself clear."

I nod and, trying to keep from saying or doing anything I'll be sorry for, I begin making my way toward my bedroom.

"We're still on for the morning," she calls out.

"On for what?" I pause with my hand on my doorknob.

"You know, we need to get some more film for the wedding episode."

"Oh ... right." I nod, suddenly feeling sleepy. Or maybe I just want to escape this craziness.

"Fran will meet us in the studio at eight."

So I promise to be ready to leave here by seven, then go into my room and close the door. And, okay, I guess I should be happy that this thing has been resolved ... or sort of resolved. But I still feel seriously irked. And hurt. I feel like my sister should apologize to me. Okay, I realize that, in her weird twisted way of thinking, she might actually believe she's done nothing wrong. But the way she's treated me was insulting and selfish and hurtful—and unless she figures it out, I don't really see how we can work together. At least without some horrible sisterly catfight, which the viewers might like.

As I get ready for bed, I realize that I probably need a slight attitude adjustment myself. Perhaps even a big one. But as I open my Bible—part of my adjustment strategy—I'm still resenting that I'm the one who always has to make these amends. I wish that Paige, the "older" sister, would take more responsibility for maintaining good relations with me for a change. Of course, I know that's not likely to happen anytime soon. And, not for the first time, I'm reminded of how God always takes the first step toward us ... he's the one who initiates reconciliation. I know I should be honored to be able to do the same. But the truth is, I'm going to need some help. A whole lot of help!

Chapter 10

"*This is from Helen,*" *Fran hands me an* envelope as Paige and I are getting makeup and hair done at the studio.

"Uh-oh," Shauna says in a teasing tone. "Hope it's not a pink slip."

I frown as I open the envelope.

"Stop making that nasty scowl," she scolds as I unfold the note from Helen. "You'll ruin your eyeliner. Not only that, but you'll need Botox before you're thirty."

My face muscles relax as I begin to read the memo.

Dear Jiminy:

As you know, we've settled on the contract. I wanted to call you this morning, but I have an early appointment, so this must suffice. This is what I want from you: Be yourself on the show. Fran will support this direction. But it must also come from you. We understand that Paige is the star, but you are the costar and we want you to let your personality shine. Don't be afraid to push

things—even if big sister doesn't like it. This is what
makes for good TV. If I have not been clear, please feel
free to call me later in the day.

Best,
Helen Hudson
Executive Producer, On the Runway

I refold the memo and return it to the envelope with a smile. So this is Helen's open invitation for me to be both seen and heard. I'm glad she actually put it in writing.

"Good news?" Shauna asks as she brushes on some blush.

"Kind of."

"Let me guess ... you're getting a raise?"

"Something like that," I tell her. And in a way it's true. It's like Helen is trying to raise my position in the show. I have to appreciate that.

Naturally, I don't mention my memo to Paige, and she seems oblivious as we ride over to our first appointment. It's with the new bridal-wear designer Fran said is supposed to be so great, but unfortunately it turns out to be a bit of a disappointment. Not that his designs are bad. In fact, I think some are rather nice. But the poor man has absolutely no camera appeal, and despite the fact that our show would give him some good, free publicity, he pretty much blows it and I suspect his footage will end up on the cutting-room floor.

Next we head over to Vera Wang. Then, with cameras rolling, Paige and I start checking out Vera's gorgeous designs. This designer definitely gets it when it comes to high-fashion weddings.

I don't mind trying on some bridesmaid dresses, but I draw the line at wedding gowns. Call me old-fashioned or a stick in the mud (like Paige is doing today) but I am not about to try on a bridal gown. Not until I'm planning my own wedding, and I don't see that happening any time soon. But Paige has no problem trying on several gowns, like she wants to test fate. And, of course, she looks absolutely amazing in them. I wouldn't be surprised if someone doesn't invite her to pose for a cover of a bridal magazine after our show airs.

"You'll make a gorgeous bride!" The woman assisting Paige adjusts a short veil that is supposed to be reminiscent of the fifties.

"Who's the lucky guy?" I tease my sister.

"Wouldn't *you* like to know." Paige tosses me a sideways glance, which I know is meant for the camera but still feels like a personal jab.

"That's right." Ignoring the prick, I speak confidentially to the camera. "Sister of the bride and I don't even know who the groom is." I hold up my hands and look down at the pale blue dress I'm modeling. "Chances are I won't even be invited to participate in the wedding."

"Not if you're wearing *those* shoes anyway." Paige turns up her nose at my sensible sandals. Naturally, I neglected to pick up some wedding-appropriate footwear from the studio this morning and Paige is not letting me, or the viewers, forget this.

"At least I can walk in these shoes," I tell her. "I mean without injuring myself anyway." I turn to the camera again. "I wonder if our viewers realize that high heels are a real health threat. Besides the possibility of broken ankles or serious foot injuries, high heels can cause chronic back and knee problems and—"

"But that all depends on the design of the shoe," Paige

injects with a confident smile. "You see ... there's a perfect high heel for everyone."

"Says who?" I ask a bit defiantly. After all, Helen told me to be myself and Fran seems to be looking on with approval.

"Every foot is different," Paige explains to me. She turns to the camera. "Seriously, fashion friends, unless you're over forty, you don't need to switch over to orthopedic shoes just yet. Don't let my little sister scare you into sacrificing style for boring sensibility." She points to my shoes, which I must admit do look a bit odd with the gown, and the cameras follow. "Seriously, do you want to go around looking like that?" She laughs.

So I hunch over, acting like I've injured my back. "Or would you rather go around like this?" I ask as I limp about, acting like I'm really messed up, and groaning with each step. "Because this is what could happen if you keep wearing overly tall high heels."

Paige laughs louder now. "Oh, that's a good look, Erin. Maybe our viewers will understand that good posture is essential to good style. You're making a perfect example of fashion don'ts today."

I stand up straight and force a smile. "I just wanted to give our viewers a visual aid—something to take with them the next time they're tempted to buy four-inch heels."

"Speaking of harmful foot health." Paige turns her attention back to the cameras. "I'll bet you don't know what can really mess up your feet." She looks back at me. "Do you know, Erin?"

"Besides high heels?"

"Yes." She has that catty smile again. "In fact, I'll give you a clue. This is one of your favorite forms of footwear."

"What?"

"*Flip-flops.*" She looks smugly back at the camera. "That's right, girls and boys, I said flip-flops. I just read an article about it." She chuckles. "Not only are flip-flops a big fashion flop, they are very bad for your feet."

"How's that?" I ask.

"For starters, unless you wear these fair-weather friends only in your home, you are literally exposing your feet to hundreds of thousands of germs and bacteria." She makes a face. "Eww. Imagine all that crud accumulating on your sweet little tootsies. I am talking about some serious germs too—some that are too nasty to even mention on this show."

"Oh, come on," I challenge her. "What could be that bad?"

"Think about it, Erin. Where do you walk in flip-flops? Bathrooms and parks and beaches and all sorts of places where disgusting things happen. You carry those things in the soles of your flip-flops and on your feet. I'm not kidding. They are seriously gross." She makes a face.

And, okay, I'm feeling a little speechless. Not that it matters, since my sister's gift of gab is fully kicked into gear.

"Not only that, but I want you to think about what some of you do with those flip-flops . . . think about where you store them when you're not wearing them. Some of you—and you know who you are—actually tote them around in your *handbags.*" She firmly shakes her head. "Unless you have them sealed safely in a plastic bag, that is a great big no-no. Trust me, you so do not want those nasty flip-flop germs residing right next to your favorite lip gloss."

"Are you serious?" Now I'm wondering where she finds this stuff.

"Absolutely."

"So maybe everyone should start washing their flip-flops," I suggest. "I mean, what's so difficult about that?"

She shrugs. "Well, here's some more breaking news. Did you know that besides the germ factor, flip-flops are dangerous in another way too? Are you aware that flip-flops are responsible for thousands, maybe millions, of falls that result in serious injuries?"

"Serious injuries?" I question.

"Do the research. Besides that, flip-flops are not good for your feet in general. They offer no support and are really hard on arches. So no matter how you look at it, flip-flops are a big flop." She shakes her finger. "And, in this girl's opinion, they are a big fashion *don't*."

I hold up my hands, making an incredulous face. "Who knew?"

"Now you do." Paige smiles brightly as Fran gives us the sign to wrap this up. "And that is why you tune into my show, because I'm your style expert. This is Paige Forrester for *On the Runway*, and I want to remind you to put your best foot forward—not in flip-flops either. As for me, that would be Prada today! I'll see you next week in London, England, where we will be enjoying Mayfair in May!"

After we've changed from the bridal wear and are walking back to our cars, I ask Paige what "Mayfair in May" is supposed to mean.

"Don't you do any research for our show?" she asks with a dismayed expression that I'm sure is for Fran's sake.

"I try to do some," I assure her, "but as you just told the viewers, this is *your* show. I don't see the need for me to be the expert."

"Mayfair is the fashion district in London," Fran tells me.

"It's where we'll be staying—in fact, we're booked in the May Fair Hotel, which actually makes for a pretty good story, not to mention a great place to stay."

"And since it's May," Paige says smugly, "'Mayfair in May' seemed appropriate. Do you get it now?"

I let out an exasperated sigh. "Why don't you save your denigration of me for when the cameras are rolling?"

Fran chuckles. "Too bad they're not rolling now."

The remainder of the week was spent going to planning sessions for the London trip, previewing episodes for the next couple of weeks, and generally avoiding conversations with my sister. I tell myself that Paige and I are just having one of those sisterly snits, and that we will get past this, but the night before we're scheduled to fly out of LAX, a part of me is starting to get worried. When I go to tell Mom goodnight, I mention it.

She nods sadly. "I've noticed you two seem a little out of sorts."

"I'm sure it'll blow over," I say. "Well, unless it just blows up."

She pats her bed. "Want to talk?"

I sigh as I sit down. "I'm so frustrated," I admit. "I mean, I feel like I'm trying, but it's like Paige always wants to do the one-up thing with me. Like she thinks I've suddenly turned into her key competitor."

"Maybe she does."

I nod. "Yeah, maybe so. She kind of reminds me of this model we've had some run-ins with." I tell Mom a little about Eliza and how everything with her is a big competition. "That gets so old."

"I know what you mean. There's a woman at work who's like that. It can be exhausting."

"Exactly."

"I usually tell myself that it's because Arden is having some self-esteem issues," Mom confides. "But the truth is that Arden is gorgeous and smart and, as far as I can see, she should be nothing but confident."

"But she's not?"

Mom shakes her head. "No. And, unfortunately, she often has the need to boost her confidence at the expense of others."

"Why is that?" I look at Mom, hoping she has the answer or maybe some kind of magic button.

"I wish I knew."

I frown. "You don't?"

"All I can say is that there's one thing that usually smoothes over the rough spots."

"What?"

"Just being extra nice to her, giving her compliments, commending her for a job well done ... you know the drill."

I stare at Mom now, trying to make sense of something that I've been exposed to for as long as I can remember—a game of sorts that I was taught to play long ago. Sometimes it feels as if I'll be playing it all my life. "So ... what if you're only contributing to her bad behavior?" I ask.

Mom looks surprised. "What?"

"What if being nice and giving compliments is simply a form of enablement?"

Mom looks amused. "Enablement?"

I nod. "I've read about this. Enablement is doing something that allows another person to continue in a harmful or destructive behavior. It's a form of codependency."

Mom laughs. "I thought your major was going to be film, not psychology."

"Psychology and film are related, don't you think?"

She nods. "Yes. I'm sure you're right."

"Anyway, what if you've done such a good job enabling Paige, as well as your friend at work, that they get stuck in some bad habits? Do you feel any responsibility for that?"

Mom's brow creases. "I suppose I should."

"But you don't?"

"Okay." She looks at me. "I will take some responsibility for your sister. I realize that your dad and I both probably spoiled her some. But we did it for the welfare of the family, Erin. And for you."

"Really?"

"So many times it was just not worth it to allow Paige to throw a fit that would ruin something for everyone. I know you understand this."

I'm feeling a little irritated. "So the princess throws a fit and everyone comes running to make it better, and this helps the princess how?"

Mom smiles. "To become even more spoiled?"

"Bingo."

"You do the same thing with Paige, Erin."

"Because I've been trained to do the same thing."

Mom makes kind of a helpless little sigh. "Here's the truth, Erin. Your dad and I never claimed to be child-rearing experts. We figured if we took care of your basic needs, loved you, and tried to offer forms of enrichment, you girls would be okay." She smiles as she runs her hand over my hair and then rests it on my cheek. "I'd say we didn't do half bad either."

For her sake, I force a smile. "Yeah, you guys did great."

Mom hugs me now. "Oh, Erin. You were always such a serious little girl. Unfortunately, you probably got that from me." She holds me out and looks at my face. "That's why I think you should understand that people like us—ones who tend to take life a bit too seriously—actually need others like Paige. We need their brightness . . . their lightness. And sometimes we have to take a little bit of selfishness with it. It's a package deal."

I nod like I get this. And, okay, I mostly get it. But I still think I'm right about the enablement thing. Paige has been enabled and encouraged to be fairly self-centered and spoiled. And, sure, she might be Little Miss Sunshine when she gets her way, but like the weather, she can turn on you. So, once again, I suppose it's my job to help make sure that things continue to go her way during our stay in London. What's new?

Chapter 11

Why am I not surprised when Benjamin insists on driving Paige to the airport? Since they arrive right before Fran and me, we get to witness the scene as paparazzi swarm Benjamin's SUV. Because the photographers are on foot, I have to wonder how they got there so quickly. Did someone tip them off? Or do they just hang out at LAX twenty-four/seven, waiting for a celeb to show so they can snap something? It reminds me of sharks in a feeding frenzy. Even though Paige Forrester and Benjamin Kross aren't the hottest Hollywood couple to be caught together, I'm sure that some of these photos will score some fairly big bucks when the paparazzi sell them to whatever gossip magazine is currently buying.

Paige and Benjamin are acting oblivious as he helps her unload her sleek Louis Vuitton bags. I have to chuckle to myself as I remember her old set of pink luggage, which was donated to Goodwill when she replaced it a few months ago. Of course, she wouldn't be caught dead with those Malibu Barbie bags now that she's a star.

Paige, impeccably dressed in Armani, removes her Gucci shades and poses for the cameras, making a sparkling smile that I'm sure she hopes will grace the cover of something. Benjamin acts a bit more subdued, almost as if he's embarrassed by this attention, which I seriously doubt. Then Paige actually pauses to answer questions.

"Where are you two going?" someone calls out.

"It's only me going," Paige answers sweetly. "Ben just offered me a ride today. I'm on my way to London to tape some *On the Runway* episodes and to make a guest appearance on *Britain's Got Style*."

"But you two are back together?"

"We're good friends," Paige says innocently. "Ben's been through a rough patch and friends help each other." She turns and pats Benjamin on the cheek. "Don't they?"

He flashes one of his famous "Hollywood" smiles and nods. "Yeah . . . good friends stick together."

Fran and I are joining them and Ben kisses Paige on the cheek. He tells her to have a good time as the paparazzi take a few more shots of us going into the terminal.

"That was fun," Paige says lightly as we go to check our bags.

"Fun?" I glance at her curiously.

"Oh, come on," she says to me. "Don't tell me you don't enjoy the attention just a little, Erin?"

I shrug. "I guess I see it as a necessary evil."

Fran chuckles. "I see it as free advertising."

It's not long before we're checked in and waiting for our plane to board. Paige, as usual, purchases an armload of the latest fashion magazines at the newsstand, which she will skim through and then leave on the plane. As we're sitting at the gate, I can feel eyes on us. Several girls have spotted Paige and they approach hesitantly, asking for autographs. When she complies, they also take photos with their phones and I can see one girl is already sending a picture—to who knows how many people. I suspect Mollie will soon be spying these same shots on whichever social network is most popular these days.

I can see that Paige, who acts nonchalant as she patiently smiles for the shots, is totally eating this up. It's like she never gets tired of the attention. I just don't get it. Yes, I understand the need for publicity and being polite to fans. But doesn't she care about privacy? Doesn't she have any boundaries when it comes to being approached by strangers? Yet again, I wonder how we can be sisters and be so totally different.

Finally, and thankfully, first class is boarding and I'm relieved to escape the little fan club. Paige blows them kisses as we head on our way and reminds them to tune in to the show.

"I won't miss that," I say as I find my seat by the window.

"What do you mean?" Paige asks as she arranges her carry-on and then sits down beside me.

"I mean in London. I won't miss the fans or the paparazzi."

She frowns. "Are you serious?"

"Huh?"

"You honestly thought there would be no paparazzi in London?"

"There weren't any in Paris. Not much anyway."

She gives me a patronizing smile. "Little sister ... you have so much to learn."

"You honestly think there'll be paparazzi in London who want to follow us?" I question.

She nods. "I'd be disappointed if there weren't."

I just shrug, then open my Birkin bag to retrieve my book, a biography of the famous director John Ford. But as I search the spaces of the bag, I realize that it's not here. I must've left it on my nightstand at home. I let out an angry growl and close my bag.

"What is it now?" Paige asks me.

"My book." I scowl. "I forgot it."

"Here." She hands me one of her fashion magazines. "Read this. It'll probably do you more good anyway."

"Right …" But I take the magazine and begin to flip through the glossy pages, frowning at the perfectly airbrushed images of overly thin models and wondering—for the ump-teenth time—how I managed to get pulled into an industry like this. A few minutes into the flight, I finally manage to find an article between some ads, and I'm actually rather intrigued by the title: "Are You an Attention Junkie? What Will You Do to Win Praise from Others?"

I glance at Paige then continue to read. Honestly, it's like they know my sister and are writing about her. The more I read, the more I realize that Paige could be seriously at risk.

"You should take this little quiz," I tell her after the flight attendant serves us coffee and scones.

"A fashion quiz?" she says with interest.

"Kind of," I say.

"Okay." She nods. "Give it to me."

I grab a pen and begin to read through the questions, circling the answers as she gives them to me. But after several questions, Paige catches on. "I thought you said it was a fash-ion quiz," she tells me.

I hold up the cover of the publication. "It's a fashion magazine," I say. "I just assumed it's somehow related to style." I continue, reading the next question, which is about where a person might stand in a crowded room of strangers.

"That would be C," she tells me. "In the center, of course,"

"Of course." I nod as if I'd do the same, although I know I would pick D, 'near an exit'.

Finally we are done and I'm tallying up her score.

"So how did I do?" she asks.

"Pretty much like I expected," I confess as I figure out which category she's fallen into.

She leans over to see, but I close the magazine. "Come on, Erin," she pesters. "What kind of test was it? How did I score?"

"It was just for fun," I tell her.

"Okay, that was fun. Now explain."

"It was a test about whether or not you might be an attention addict."

"You mean like ADD?" she asks. "I was evaluated for attention deficit disorder as a kid, you know, but they didn't think I have it. They decided I was restless and energetic."

"No, it's not that kind of attention," I explain. "It's not a deficit disorder. It's more like an addiction."

"An addiction?" She frowns. "What do you mean?"

"The psychologist who wrote the article claims that some people can be addicted to attention."

"What?"

"It's like a drug for them. They can't get enough. They'll do anything to get praise and approval from others."

She makes a face. "That sounds desperate ... and pathetic."

I don't know how to respond to this, so I just nod.

"So, how did I score?"

"Well, the author had five categories ..." Now I'm wishing

I hadn't done this. What good will it do? Most likely it'll only aggravate her.

"What were the categories?" Paige breaks off a piece of scone and nibbles on it.

"I, uh, I can't remember." My fingers curl around the edges of the magazine and I'm wishing I could open the window and just chuck it out.

"Oh, come on, Erin." She gives me an irate look. "It's my magazine anyway. Do I have to pry it out of your fingers?"

"No."

"Then *tell* me. What are the categories, and how did I score?"

"But it might make you mad."

She gives me a sugary smile. "I promise I won't get mad at you, Erin. Now you've got me really curious. I want to know what kind of pathetic people get addicted to attention."

I take in a deep breath and open the magazine, deciding to read them to her backward. "The five categories are: One, the Hermit Crab—you stay as far away from others as possible and if they come your way, you snap at them. Two, the Mole—you use false humility to pretend you don't like the limelight, but you secretly crave it. Three, the Cat—attention is no big deal, you can take it or leave it, but mostly you just want to live your life. Four, the Dog—you adore attention and eagerly pursue it with tail a-wagging." I pause to clear my throat. "And five, the Peacock—you live for attention, you can't get enough, and you will strut your stuff until your feathers fall off to obtain it."

"And . . . so?" Paige waits.

"So what?"

"Which one am I?" She smiles sweetly.

"You mean you don't know?"

She glares at me now. "Do you know how aggravating you can be sometimes?"

"You're the peacock," I say quickly. "A perfect score."

She frowns. "The peacock?"

I nod and continue reading the article.

"Well ..." She sighs. "At least peacocks are the prettiest ones in that quiz. I wouldn't want to be a hermit crab or a mole."

I can't help but laugh since that's exactly a peacock sort of response.

"So which one are you?" she asks.

"I didn't take the test."

"Well, take it then because I'm sure you're the hermit crab."

I roll my eyes. "I'm pretty sure I'm the cat. But if it makes you happy I'll take it."

"No, you'd probably just cheat. So does it say anything else about the peacock?"

"Yeah, most of the article is aimed at the peacock."

"Why?"

"Because the peacock is the serious attention addict."

Paige shakes her head. "No ... I don't think so."

"You don't?"

"No. I think whoever wrote that article didn't understand peacocks. Peacocks get attention simply because they can. It's the way they're made. I mean, you wouldn't expect a peacock to go around hiding in a hole or trying to keep people from looking at her beautiful feathers. The nature of the peacock is to be the center of attention. Everyone enjoys looking at a peacock."

"Right." I nod and return to reading. Fortunately Paige returns to her magazine too. And, although I'm surprised at how dense my sister is, I begin to realize as I continue to read the article that it's like a blind spot with her. She doesn't have any idea that she's an attention addict. And it sounds like she won't get it either — not until certain things happen.

The article lists various circumstances that might help an addict move toward recovery — things like suddenly being shoved out of the limelight due to unfortunate circumstances like illness or injury or financial difficulties. Or she might literally exhaust herself and her resources while seeking the limelight. Last but not least, she might come to the realization that all the attention in the world will never satisfy her. It seems that, like with other addictions, the first step to getting better is to admit you have a problem. Since I don't see that happening with Paige anytime soon, I won't be holding my breath.

But after I finish the article I realize that peacocks like Paige don't get there alone. Their hunger for attention combined with their narcissistic nature drives them to surround themselves with friends, fans, and even the occasional stalker. They crave for their followers to adore them and constantly shower them with praise and attention. Without those faithful admirers, a peacock will perish.

It's not that I want Paige to perish. But I wouldn't mind if the peacock in my sister turned it down a notch or two. This is for Paige's sake as much as for mine, because it sounds like peacocks eventually suffer from serious burnout. The article lists a number of celebrities who've gone to desperate measures to keep the spotlight on them even though their careers were clearly over. It's not pretty. I hate to think of my sister ending up like that.

Yet it seems the only thing I can do to help her—and it's not much—is to make sure I'm not one of those people that constantly feeds her addiction with my praise and adoration. Not that I want to do that, but I know I've often fallen into that pattern simply because it's my easy way out. But lately it seems like I don't care anymore, like I'm rubbing Paige the wrong way on purpose.

So maybe that's it; maybe I'm the antidote for Paige's attention addiction. Or maybe I'm only fooling myself. For all I know I could be the mole—the one who secretly craves attention almost as much as a peacock. Just to be sure, I take the test. To my relief, unless I cheated (and I tried not to), I am the cat. Attention is no big deal ... I can take it or leave it. Of course, like a finicky cat, I want attention when I want it ... and I don't want attention when I don't want it. And, as the article points out, life is seldom like that. Especially mine.

Chapter

12

It's the next morning when we arrive at Heathrow. Although I slept somewhat during the flight, I feel frazzled and frumpy as we walk through the terminal, but Paige looks like she just stepped out of makeup and hair, which is handy because the camera crew arrived in London yesterday. Right after we pick up our bags and pass through customs, they start filming us.

As always, Fran hangs behind the scenes as the cameras roll, but I don't get that luxury as Paige and I (just two American girls) casually stroll through Heathrow making our official arrival in London look like we think we're Brad and Angelina. I try not to feel conspicuous as a crowd of curious onlookers watches our progression. But I wish I'd thought to check my hair ... not to mention my teeth. I obviously did not study my schedule carefully because I really thought we'd have time to go to our hotel and freshen up a bit before launching into shooting today.

"Here are my tips for arriving fresh and lovely after an overnight flight," Paige says to the cameras as we pause near the exit. "First off, drink plenty of water to avoid puffy eyes." She points to me and giggles. "Apparently somebody forgot to do this. Next, remember to remove your makeup and apply moisturizer before falling asleep so your skin will wake up looking refreshed. Then be sure to give yourself time to apply some fresh makeup before the plane lands." She looks at me and dismally shakes her head. "Notice these raccoon eyes from yesterday's mascara. Well, a little moisturizer and tissue could've cleaned that right up."

"Thanks for telling me now," I say with a stiff smile.

"And here's a tip for avoiding this little disaster." She actually turns me around so the camera can see the back of my head. "Oh, my!" She giggles. "To prevent serious bed head like this, try wrapping a silk scarf loosely around your hair before you fall asleep on the plane. It will keep your hair in place and looking coifed when you make your arrival."

As I turn around and touch the back of my head, I can feel that it's flat and messy. Big surprise there. Then as we head outside to the passenger pickup area, Paige is telling the cameras about how she packed a couple of extra clothing items in her carry-on. "So I could do a quick presto change-o and not have to stand here on this lovely sunny morning looking like I slept on the street." She turns to me. "Unfortunately my sister was not as well prepared." She shrugs and smiles for the camera. "Oh, well. Maybe next time." Then she waves her arms dramatically. "Welcome to London, England, where we will soon discover what makes Brit fashion sizzle."

"That's a wrap," Fran calls out. "Nice work, Paige."

Paige grins at me. "Thanks for being such a good little example of the fashion-on-the-go don'ts. You make my work so easy."

I suppress the urge to growl. "I'm sure your fans will appreciate seeing your true colors, Paige. The way you treat your sister must endear yourself to them ever so much."

She gives me a puzzled frown.

"There's our limo, girls." Fran points to a black car, then goes over to consult with the crew. With relief I hurry over to the car, but Paige is suddenly besieged by the small crowd that has been watching her. Naturally, she is in her element as she cheerfully poses for photos and signs her name on whatever pieces of paper are shoved her way. Eventually Fran pulls her away from her adoring fans and ushers her over to the limo.

"So you thought there'd be no paparazzi in London," Paige says as she slides in next to me.

"I wouldn't exactly call curious onlookers paparazzi," I point out.

"Don't be too sure," she says as she removes a compact from her bag, opens it, and checks out her already-immaculate appearance. "A couple of those cameras looked fairly serious to me."

I'm looking over my notes for our trip now and I realize that there really isn't anything in here about being filmed upon our arrival, but when I point this out to Fran she tells me it was a last-minute change. "Didn't Paige tell you before we left?" Fran asks.

"Obviously not."

Fran laughs. "Oh . . . I think I see why."

"So this was a little set-up to make me into your fashion don't?" I glare at my sister. "Real nice."

"Hey, I could've told you to fix yourself up," she says, "but would you have given up your precious sleep to do it?"

I consider this. I had finally been sleeping soundly just before the flight touched down.

"Besides, according to that survey, you're the one who doesn't care about being in the spotlight, right?"

I just shrug as I search in my bag for something to improve my appearance — like that's even possible.

"Why should you care about how you look then?"

"Oh, Paige." Fran shakes her head with disapproval. "That's not very nice of you."

"But it's true."

"I'm sorry you were caught off guard," Fran tells me. "Paige thought our viewers would enjoy hearing some tips about how you can travel and arrive in style. I had no idea she didn't tell you."

"Don't forget," Paige holds up her index finger, "this is a reality show. I was merely trying to keep it real for the sake of the viewers."

I carefully measure my words now, trying not to lose my temper as I respond to my sister's trickster ways. "Well ... for the sake of the show, and since it *is* a show about fashion and style, I would think you'd want your own sister to put her best foot forward too. After all, if your costar looks bad, doesn't it reflect poorly on you as the queen of style — like, oops, you missed something?"

Fortunately this seems to stump my sister. Without saying a word, she turns away from me, looking out the window as I continue to forage through my bag. Finally I find a scruffy-looking tube of lip gloss and smear some on my chapped lips.

"I spoke to Shauna and Luis at the airport," Fran tells me. "They'll meet us at the hotel and we should have plenty of time to work you over before our next shoot so that you'll be perfectly presentable."

"Thanks." I run a hand through my messy bed-head hair and sigh. "It's nice to know that *someone* in the show cares."

"Okay, girls," Fran begins in a firm voice. "This is a reality show. We do want you to be yourselves, including sisterly squabbles if necessary, but you also need to bear in mind we have a number of shows to film in London. That means *everyone* does their part to make them a success. Right, Paige?"

Paige turns to us with what seems a pleasant expression, except that I can see a glint of mean in those big blue eyes. "Of course. You know I always deliver my very best for the show."

Fran nods. "Yes. I just wanted to be sure we were all on the same page now."

"Meaning no more surprises?" I aim this to Paige and she smiles like she's got all kinds of clever things tucked up those designer sleeves.

"Oh, there should always be some surprises," she says in a catty tone. "What would be the fun if there weren't?"

Fran chuckles and I look out the window, taking in the British scenery and hoping there will be time to shoot some photos myself. As we drive, Fran points out some places of interest, including several museums. "And that's Harrods," she points out my window.

"What's Harrods?" I ask as I peer out on what looks like a castle.

"*What's Harrods?*" Paige repeats sarcastically as she leans over to see better. "Just the most magnificent department store in the world." She sighs. "We are going there, right?"

"Yes, definitely. It's on the schedule."

I blink in disbelief at the huge castle-like structure. "*That* is a department store?"

"Nearly five acres of lovely shopping all under one amazing roof." Paige looks smitten. "Oh, it'll be like dying and going to heaven."

I make a face. "I sure hope heaven is better than a humungous department store." I shake my head. "How can one store be nearly five acres? That's just crazy."

"Crazy good." Paige sighs again and I wonder if she's about to swoon.

A few minutes pass and Fran is pointing out where Hyde Park is and then explaining how we are now on Piccadilly and coming into the fashion district. "If this were actually Fashion Week," she says, "it would be packed. As it is, we were able to get a pretty great suite with adjoining rooms in the May Fair Hotel."

"Will we be able to stay there during the next London Fashion Week too?" Paige asks hopefully.

"Leah is working on it." Fran checks her phone now. "Fortunately September is still a ways off. Let's just focus on this London trip, okay?" She points to the right. "That's Green Park," she tells us. "Buckingham Palace Gardens are just beyond."

"So is Buckingham Palace there too?"

"No," Paige tells me in her most sarcastic voice. "They only have a garden, Erin. No palace. The queen has to camp out there when she's in town."

Fran laughs while I roll my eyes and wonder if Paige took mean pills this morning. A drizzly rain is starting to fall as our driver meanders through the heavy traffic, but it's coming down hard by the time Fran points out the hotel down the street.

"I thought you said this wasn't the busy time of year," I say to Fran as our limo pulls onto the end of a fairly long line of cars, which are dropping guests off at the front entrance.

"Well, there are a few fashion shows this week," she admits. "I suppose that might account for the traffic. That and the weather. Everyone probably wants to be dropped off at the door."

I stare at the non-moving line of cars ahead of us. "This looks like it could take awhile. Do you think we should just get out and make a run for it?"

"Seeing that we're due at Burberry at two thirty and we still need to get you through hair, makeup, and wardrobe — that's not a bad idea." Fran turns to Paige. "I suppose you can ride on up to the front door if you want to make a queenly entrance and stay dry, but Erin and I will hoof it. I wish I had taken my umbrella out of my suitcase."

Paige frowns. "You're going out in the rain?"

"The entrance is like fifty feet from here," I tell her as I scramble to grab my purse and carry-on. Fran shoots the driver some instructions for dropping off our luggage and picking us up at one o'clock, and then pops out and starts running toward the entrance.

"Okay," Paige says reluctantly. "I guess I'll come with you too."

I wait for Paige to gather her things and then we both spurt out of the limo, dashing through the rain until we reach the protection of the portico, which is crowded with other guests trying to emerge from cars and gather bags as they avoid the wet weather. Fran seems to have already made her way inside.

"There's Paige Forrester," someone calls out, and the next thing we know several people, as well as some cameras, are clamoring around us. I cannot believe the British paparazzi are here—or that they even know who my sister is. Naturally, Paige's eyes light up and, in one movement, she gives her head a quick shake and fluffs her damp hair to instant perfection, breaking out into a smile so sunny I almost expect the clouds to part.

"I'm Claire Kelly of *London Star Watch*." A pretty dark-haired woman hands Paige a card. "Do you have a moment for a quick interview for tonight's show?"

"Certainly." Paige nods congenially. She doesn't even look surprised and I almost wonder if she might've been the one to tip off the press. But why should they care?

"I understand you're here to appear on *Britain's Got Style*," Claire says to Paige. As her camera guy begins filming, several others draw in closer, snapping photos or holding up mics like this is the story of the year. It must be a slow day for the London press if these people have no more-newsworthy items to cover.

"That's right," Paige tells her. "Our show *On the Runway* was invited to participate in a *Britain's Got Style* episode, and I am honored to assist as a judge."

"And what qualifies you, a relatively young American girl, to judge British style?" a middle-aged woman asks in a snooty tone.

Paige lets out a tinkle of a laugh. "Oh, that's a great question. I realize I am rather young, but I seem to have an innate sense of style that our American viewers can relate to. Our show has experienced a growing popularity both in the States and abroad." She ignites her most engaging smile. "I guess it's hard to explain ... *je ne sais quoie.*"

"How long will your show be in London, Paige?" Claire

asks pleasantly, as if she wants to apologize for the other woman.

"We expect to wrap up—"

"Never mind that," a man behind Claire interrupts. "What Brits really want to know is—are you and Benjamin Kross in a relationship?"

"Benjamin and I are friends and I've—"

"But isn't it true that you were seen *shopping for wedding gowns?*" another woman calls out. "Are you planning to *marry* Benjamin Kross?"

"What about the criminal charges against Benjamin Kross?" the earlier guy persists like a bulldog. "Isn't he going to go to prison for the murder of Mia Renwick, his deceased costar from *Malibu Beach*?"

"The charges against Benjamin have been dropped," Paige says in a stiff voice that's quickly losing its warmth. "The investigation revealed that a number of factors contributed to the—uh—the automobile accident."

"And there's been a settlement." I offer this morsel of information to relieve a bit of the pressure from Paige and hopefully to get us out of here. "Mia Renwick's family agreed to drop the civil charges. I'm surprised you haven't heard about this by now. A special *Malibu Beach* episode aired recently with Benjamin explaining what actually happened that night." I'm tugging on Paige's arm, trying to move us toward the entrance and out of this British media feeding frenzy.

"That's the younger sister," someone else says and—great—the cameras are all pointing at me now.

"We need to go prepare for a show," I say loudly. "Please, excuse—"

"So what about those wedding plans?" The bulldog guy

steps in front of Paige. "Are you and Benjamin planning to marry now that Mia is out of the picture?"

"Yes, please tell us *why* you were trying on wedding gowns!" a female voice calls out.

"Seems a bit hasty to be tying the knot with a young man barely cleared of murder charges," someone comments.

Without answering, Paige looks at me with worried eyes, like she's blanking out or about to have some kind of panic attack. So, still holding on to her arm, I go ahead and field this question too.

"We tried on wedding gowns for an upcoming episode of our show," I yell above the crowd that's getting noisier, tugging on Paige's arm, which is futile since we're enclosed on all sides now. "The show will air in early June and—"

"I want a word with Paige Forrester," a short man with a dark beard yells as he muscles his way through the crowd. He steps up and shakes a newspaper at Paige. "So you're the Yank who thinks she's going to tell us Brits how to have style?" He holds up what appears to be a British tabloid. "Have you seen this? It's hot off the press and something that should interest everyone here."

I stare at the grainy photograph, which appears to be of me and Paige, but I cannot for the life of me remember when or where it was taken. In the picture I'm standing by a white baby crib, holding a teddy bear, and Paige is on the other side of the crib with a startled expression on her face. The headline reads: "A Pregnant Paige Forrester Arrives in London to Teach Brits about Style."

"Pregnant?" I turn and stare at Paige.

Her face pales and she slowly shakes her head. "That's not true."

"Who's the father?" a woman calls out. "Benjamin Kross?"

"That baby should be some looker then," someone comments with laughter. "Paige Forrester and Benjamin Kross having a baby together! There'll be good money for whoever captures those baby pictures."

I grab the tabloid and stare closely at the photo. Something about it is familiar, but then I realize it's not what it seems. "This photo has been tampered with," I yell out over the new flood of baby comments and questions. "Yes, that's me standing next to a baby crib, but I was shopping with a friend—*not Paige*. I was with my friend who actually is pregnant. But someone must have taken a photo of Paige and stuck it on right here to make it look like a big story." I shove the paper back at the man now. "Why anyone believes this kind of trash—or spends money on it—is beyond me."

"I am not pregnant," Paige says stiffly.

"You heard her," I yell at them. "Now, please, excuse us before I call for security. Thank you for this very warm British welcome and this very lovely press conference!" And, with my hand still wrapped around Paige's arm, I drag her along behind me as I push my way through the crowd and into the hotel where Fran is standing in the middle of the lobby just shaking her head.

"Good grief," she tells us. "I thought I was going to have to call for backup. How did you manage to get caught by that group of media thugs?"

"That's what I'd like to know." I turn to look at Paige who still looks fairly rattled.

Fran's looking at Paige too. "Do you have any idea where they came from or how they knew you were staying at this hotel?"

"Well ... it is the May Fair Hotel," Paige says meekly as we proceed through the lobby. "The fashion hot spot."

"Yes, but it's not the only hotel in this neighborhood." Fran looks suspicious. "How did they know what time you were arriving?"

Paige looks nervously over her shoulder as we wait for the elevator. "I ... uh ... I thought a little publicity ... might be good."

"You really did set that up?" I ask as we step inside.

"Not exactly." She sighs.

"What do you mean not exactly?" I persist.

"Well, I suppose it kind of leaked out onto one of the social networks."

"You mean you announced to the whole world what time we were arriving in London? And where we were staying?" I stare at my sister in wonder.

She gives me a blank look that says it all.

"No more giving out specific information," Fran says as we ride up.

"But I thought publicity would be a good thing," Paige says as we emerge on our floor.

"Tabloids saying that you're pregnant with Benjamin Kross's baby and picking out wedding gowns?" I demand. "That's a good thing?"

"*What?*" Fran looks at Paige with a shocked expression.

Paige holds up her hands in a helpless gesture. "I didn't know they would take that direction ... or go that far. I didn't know they would make up vicious lies about me!"

"Don't you get it?" I ask her. "Paparazzi and tabloid reporters are like a runaway train—why would you even want to get on board?"

"Maybe I don't … not anymore." Paige makes a weak smile. "Let me off at the next stop, please."

"It might be too late to get off." Fran hands us our room keys. As I go into my room, which adjoins Paige's, I think Fran might be right. This train has left the station. Hopefully we're not heading for a serious wreck.

Chapter

13

The May Fair is a very fashionable and contemporary hotel. *Quite posh*, as Brits might say. Now some people might think "posh" simply means stylish. And people might assume it's thanks to Victoria Beckham, who went by Posh back in her Spice Girl days. But I looked up the meaning of posh and was surprised to learn the word originated in the early 1900s. The initials P.O.S.H. were used on ships traveling between India and England, standing for "Portside Out and Starboard Home," and this would be stamped onto the first class passengers' luggage so that their luggage could be switched to the appropriate side of the boat ... because first class passengers always occupied the shady side of the ship. If the story is true, this must mean that regular folks like me got to bake in the sun. But when I told Lionel my piece of trivia, he laughed and told me the story was an urban legend. True or not, I still like it.

Anyway, I'm completely pleased with my swanky hotel room and thankful I'm not sharing it with Paige. Of course, when I see Paige's digs—a large comfortable suite—I do feel a tiny twinge of jealousy. I remind myself, however, that she is the star of *On the Runway*, and I agreed to let her stay that way. After her grilling downstairs, I think she's paying dearly for her fancy accommodations.

It's not long before Luis and Shauna show up and go to work on me while Paige changes her clothes and picks out an outfit for me to wear today. Meanwhile Fran has ordered room service and when we get the chance, we take turns getting a bite to eat. Finally, I change into the somewhat conservative outfit of a khaki wool skirt and black cashmere sweater and black ankle boots. Actually, I'm pleased with the outfit, but I'm surprised Paige was okay with it since we're shooting today. Even the accessories are fairly low-key. Just a silver chain necklace, stud earrings, and a simple clasp bracelet.

"Here," she says as she hands me a khaki Burberry trench coat, complete with their trademark plaid lining.

"You look nice," I tell her as I slip on the new coat. "Is that Burberry too?" She has on a pale gray jacket and pencil skirt with a pink silk scarf tied loosely around her neck, as well as perfect accessories that, as usual, make a bit more of a statement than mine. And her shoes, gray suede ankle boots, are very chic.

She smiles and strikes a pose, then slips on a really gorgeous pale gray trench coat. "All thanks to Christopher Bailey."

"Who's that?"

"Just the reason Burberry is selling a lot more than raincoats these days."

"Well, we picked a good day to go to Burberry," I say as Fran hands us our umbrellas. Mine is plaid and Paige's is that same soft gray.

As we go down the elevator, Paige dons her oversized Gucci sunglasses and even rearranges her pale pink scarf to cover her hair, like she thinks she's disguising herself. If anything, it makes her even more striking as we walk through the lobby and I notice that a lot of heads turn to watch as she strides toward the entrance. Fortunately the throng of media freaks has disappeared, probably off to torture some other unsuspecting celeb. And, because our car is waiting, we don't even need our umbrellas.

"Chris Bailey started with Gucci," Paige informs us as we drive through town. "He's been with Burberry about ten years. He's taken some heat too."

"Taken some heat?" I question.

"Several years ago, Chris's designs, particularly the ones with the Burberry plaid, became so popular that knock-off companies started reproducing them. For some reason British gangs and street kids couldn't get enough. Their designs became part of what was called 'chav' culture, and Chris had to scramble to protect the Burberry image."

"How did he do that?" I ask as I watch London scenery flashing by. I want to ask Fran if she knows what we're passing, but Paige seems to be on a roll and I think it's probably going to help her to get into gear for this next interview.

"Mostly he had to pull way back on the plaid," she says as she checks something on her phone. "In fact, Burberry threatened to sue some automaker for producing a car that was painted in the plaid."

"You're kidding." I look at the lining of my trench coat and try to imagine a whole car painted like that.

"They called it a Chavrolet." She chuckles.

We're going over a bridge now. "Is this the Thames River?" I ask as I peer at the rather gray-looking water, which merely seems to be reflecting the gray dreary day.

"It is," Fran confirms.

"But, please, Erin," Paige says to me, "don't mention a word about the chav business when we're at Horseferry House."

"Horseferry House?"

"That's Burberry headquarters," Fran tells me as she looks up from her map. "It looks like we're almost there."

"Now, remember," Paige directs me as the car pulls up to a large structure. "This is Great Britain, where good etiquette is expected."

"What are you saying?" I ask as I reach for my Birkin bag.

"Just that manners matter."

I frown at her, but refrain from voicing my thoughts. But, seriously, does she think I'm going to pick my nose or belch or something?

This time we need to use our umbrellas, but soon we're inside where our crew is already set up and ready to go. Soon we are given the tour of what seems a never-ending building, and during a brief lull I inquire as to the size of Horseferry House.

"We're about twenty thousand square meters," our guide tells me.

"Oh ..." I nod as I attempt to convert that to square feet in my mind.

"Or for you Yanks, about one hundred and sixty thousand square feet."

"Wow, that's huge."

He just smiles in that understated British sort of way, but I can tell he likes the idea that we're impressed.

We finally wind up in the showroom and I must admit that I really do like Burberry's style. "These are exactly the kinds of clothes that I feel comfortable wearing," I say as we wait for one of the designers to join us for Paige's final interview. "Stylish but sensible."

"I like that," says a British voice from behind me. "Stylish but sensible."

I turn to see a good-looking guy coming in. Lanky and thin, he has serious eyes and his hair has that mussed-up look, but it only adds to his overall attractiveness.

"Christopher Bailey," Paige says, and with a bright smile, she moves past me to where she takes his hand. "Thank you for allowing us to visit Horseferry House today. And thank you so much for taking time to meet with us now."

"Ah, the renowned Paige Forrester." He returns her smile. "I heard we're having the American Fashion Invasion."

Paige looks slightly off guard, but quickly recovers. "Oh, we've simply come over to study British design." She tilts her head coyly. "I think we could learn a lot about style here."

He chuckles. "So you're not actually here to educate *us* then?"

"No, of course not." She shakes her head.

"I think your style is brilliant," I tell him, still trying to figure out my role in this new little game we're playing. "I was just telling Paige that you design the kinds of clothes I like to wear."

He nods. "Stylish but sensible."

"This is my sister, Erin Forrester," Paige takes the reins again.

"Tell me, Erin Forrester . . ." He studies me with curiosity. "What brought you into the world of fashion?"

"I . . . uh . . . mostly my sister," I admit.

He looks amused.

"She's the true fashionista of the family," I continue. "But

I do have some interest in fashion." Okay, this is probably an overstatement.

"Such as?"

"Well ... I care about environmentally conscious fashions," I begin. "And I appreciate creative designers who come up with new ways to communicate fashion." I glance at Paige, hoping she'll jump in now.

But he nods as if he appreciates my slightly lame contribution. "Perhaps you've heard of our foundation then ..." Naturally, I am blank.

"Oh, yes," Paige says quickly. "The Burberry Foundation." She turns to me now. "Christopher was instrumental in setting up this foundation. The purpose is to dedicate global resources to help young people realize their creative dreams. It's really a wonderful program with a focus on the future of fashion."

He looks both intrigued and impressed. "Someone's been doing her homework."

"I always appreciate hearing about designers who give back to the community," she continues, "whether local or global. Burberry does both."

Again, I can't help but be impressed with my savvy sister. Also, I'm relieved to have her back in the driver's seat. I can tell that she's pleased with herself too. She and Christopher chat amicably for a few more minutes, and then when it's time for him to go, she gracefully wraps it up.

"Nice work," Fran tells her as the cameras shut down.

"Thanks."

"You too," Fran tells me.

"Thanks," I say with less enthusiasm. "But I have a feeling that I should follow my sister's example and start doing my homework."

Paige laughs. "Oh, that's okay, Erin. You keep being your-self and I'll be me, and I think we'll be just fine."

In other words, I think she's telling me to watch out — warning me that she wants to remain in control of the show and, hey, I'm okay with that.

"Next stop is Stella McCartney," Fran informs us almost apologetically. "Sorry to pack so much into your first day but, as you know, the payoff is a free day tomorrow. The only time we could tour Stella's was after-hours today, so we decided to jump on it."

"Now here's someone I know a little about," I admit as we ride through London, where the rain has stopped and the city seems to be shining in the sunlight.

"Do tell," my sister says in a challenging tone. "I suppose you've heard of her famous father."

I give her a *duh* look. "Yes, I'm sure everyone has heard of Sir Paul McCartney from the Beatles. But not everyone knows that Stella's mother, the late Linda McCartney, was an animal rights activist and probably the reason Stella is a strict vegetar-ian and uses no fur or leather in her designs."

"Bravo." Paige nods. "Tell me more."

"Uh ..." I'm trying to remember what else I read about her when I was doing a bit of research at home. Apparently not enough. "Stella also designs sportswear for Adidas and someone else ... I think."

"Yes, as well as her own full line of clothes," Paige supple-ments. "She used to work for Chloé and Gucci. She designs for icons like Madonna and Gwyneth Paltrow and she even has a skin-care line called CARE."

"Bravo," I say back to her.

She nods in a queenly sort of way.

"You know we have a bit of time to kill before six," Fran tells us. She glances down at her map and notes then calls up to the driver. "Let's stop at Bar Italia in Soho."

"We're going to a bar?" I ask.

"A coffee bar," she tells me.

"Yes, this *is* London." Paige uses a tutorial tone. "If we wanted something more than coffee, we would go to a pub."

I roll my eyes. "Oh, yes, wise one," I say with sarcasm. "Thank you for straightening me out."

Bar Italia turns out to be an interesting place. According to Fran, it's the most popular all-night coffee bar in London. Why anyone wants to drink coffee in the middle of the night is beyond me, but I suppose some might come for the food. I'll admit it smells delicious, but since we only have about forty minutes to spare, we settle for coffees and pastries.

Then we clean crumbs from our faces and freshen our makeup, and we're off to Stella McCartney. The shop is very chic and impressive. While Paige, in top form, does a quick interview, I mostly just listen, somewhat in awe of this woman who seems much younger than her late thirties. Not only is she pretty and creative, it's like she has a youthful spirit. And, once again, I'm surprised at how much I like most of her designs. Maybe I am secretly a British fashion freak and I just never knew it before now.

But as Paige is wrapping it up, I can tell that we're all feeling pretty tired. When we return to the hotel it's past seven and all I want to do is order some room service and crash. But, once again, we are met by some media thugs as we attempt to enter our hotel.

"We don't have time for this," Fran says as they literally block the door.

Paige is back in her Gucci shades and pink scarf disguise. Very effective. I'm controlling myself from yelling at them to get out of our way.

"Just a quick question," a guy says to Paige.

"You and Benjamin Kross were—"

"Benjamin is just my friend," Paige practically shouts at him.

"But photos of you two kissing are already circulating the Internet," he continues. "And rumors of your pregnancy are—"

"I am not pregnant!"

Fran is waving to a doorman over by a taxi. "Please, call security," she yells at him.

"When is the wedding date?" another paparazzo calls out.

"Get out of our way," I shout as I push past the rude man.

Just then the doorman rushes over and takes charge, threatening the paparazzi with legal action if they don't leave. Suddenly we are free of them and inside the lobby.

"If this doesn't stop we might have to change hotels," Fran says with irritation.

Paige groans. "I'm sorry."

"Hey, maybe we can spread a new rumor," I say as we get in the elevator. "That we've switched hotels."

"Or maybe I can get a better disguise," Paige suggests as she removes her scarf and shades. "Like a long black wig."

Fran nods. "You know, that's not a bad idea."

"I suppose that means I'll need a wig too," I say without enthusiasm.

"Or else we just come and go separately," Paige says dismally.

I consider this. In some ways, I wouldn't mind separating

myself from my sister a bit. Fending off paparazzi and hearing those kinds of accusations isn't exactly fun. Especially when I'm not totally sure what is and is not actually true. I wouldn't be surprised if there really are photos of Ben and Paige kissing circulating on the Internet right now. Really, for all I know, they may be secretly planning a wedding. Not that I plan on asking Paige about this. Because, the truth is, I'm not sure I totally trust her right now. I get the feeling that not only is she protecting her place on the show, as she clearly showed me this morning with her airport ambush (and possibly her choice of clothing for me today), but that she's not being totally honest with me either.

Chapter 14

We agree to go our separate ways on our day off. Paige wants to sleep in and then do some shopping, and I want to do some typical sightseeing that she's not interested in. I decide to get an early start, but once I'm down in the lobby, I have no idea what I should do. So I consult with the concierge, a middle-aged man with wire-rimmed glasses and a neat bowtie. He reminds me of the stereotype of an English butler.

"How much time have you got?" he asks me quickly, studying his computer screen as if it's of more interest to him than I am.

"All day," I tell him.

"What are your primary interests?" He looks up from his screen and studies me closely as if trying to determine who I am and where I came from.

"I'm not sure. I do like to take photos."

"Have you any interest in Shakespeare?" he asks suddenly.

"Yes," I say eagerly. "Absolutely."

"Have you a car?"

I shake my head no.

"Are you are on your own?"

"Today I am."

"But you say you have all day?"

I nod, wondering where he's going with this inquisition.

"Then, if I were you, I'd nab a seat on the Gray Line tour of Stratford-upon-Avon."

"Gray Line? Is that a bus?"

"Yes. But I promise you, it's a good tour. You'll see Shakespeare's birthplace and Anne Hathaway's cottage. If you're at all interested in literature, I think you'll find it charming."

I'm still not sure. "It's an all-day tour?"

"Yes. If you decide right now there's a chance I can get you on it."

I'm thinking about it. Do I really want to spend the day on a bus?

"Of course, there are some Shakespearean sights one can see right here in London," he says offhandedly. "The Globe Theater and such. You can easily catch those on another day. But truly, if you want to experience Shakespeare, to walk where he walked, to see the sights that the great Bard saw, you should capitalize on this tour. Also, you might snatch some brilliant photos this time of year. Stratford-upon-Avon is spectacularly beautiful in May."

"All right." I nod. "Please see if you can get me on this tour."

He looks back down at his computer screen, clicks a few times, then picks up the phone, has a quick conversation, and finally hangs up. "You're in luck," he announces.

Soon we have it all squared away and he tells me the bus will be by to pick me up in about an hour, which gives me just enough time to sample the "full English" breakfast. I'm guessing it is rarely served in this hotel because the waiter seems delighted when I order it. This traditional meal comes complete with grilled tomatoes, mushrooms, eggs, sausages, and "rashers," which is actually bacon and rather tasty. Of course, I can't eat the whole thing and I suspect the reason they call it the "full English" breakfast is because you become quite full upon consuming it.

By the time I'm stuffed and making my way through the lobby, telling myself that now I had better skip lunch, I see the concierge waving toward me.

"Your chariot awaits," he calls out, pointing to the entrance. I thank him and wave, hurrying out the door and onto a bus that is full of—old people. Not terribly old-old, like one foot in the graveyard old, but around my grandma's age. To my surprise, they all cheer when I step onto the bus. Feeling conspicuous and wondering if I've just made a huge mistake, I give them a feeble smile and take a seat near the front.

"I hope you don't mind," a middle-aged woman seated opposite me says, "but I took the liberty to tell everyone that we've got a real celebrity on board."

I blink. "A celebrity?"

She glances down at a notepad. "You *are* Erin Forrester, correct?"

"Yes."

"That's what the concierge told me." She sticks out her hand. "I'm Harriet Barstow, your tour guide."

"Nice to meet you and thanks for waiting."

She peers curiously at me. "Now is it true that you're a star of some American television show?"

"Not exactly a star," I say quickly. "My sister, Paige Forrester, is the real star. I'm just her costar. Our show is called *On the Runway*."

"Because the other tourists, also Americans, were eager to have a young star in their midst, they tolerated your lateness just now." She smiles patiently. "But I hope you won't make a habit of it." She stands as the driver pulls out into traffic, getting her microphone ready.

"I'll do my best to keep you from waiting." I assure her.

"So, we're off now," she announces to the rest of the bus. "We welcome Erin Forrester to our group. She has informed me that her television show is called *On the Runway*. We will be traveling northwest for a bit. For our entertainment, I have a little quiz for you. Since I know you are mostly retired school teachers, I will attempt to make the questions a bit more challenging than usual." She begins to ask questions about Shakespeare, his history, his works, and even some quotes. Several of the retired teachers seem to be serious Shakespeare buffs. I even get one right when she asks who the main character's daughter was in *The Tempest*.

"Prospero's daughter was Miranda," I call out before anyone else, which wins me a Cadbury chocolate bar. I stick this in my bag for later—just in case I ever get hungry again.

It's around eleven when the bus stops in the quaint-looking town of Stratford-upon-Avon. As we get out and mill around, waiting for our tour guide, I learn that the retired teachers are all from Madison, Wisconsin. It seems they are mostly women, and for the most part seem very chatty and friendly. A few, to my surprise, have actually seen *On the Runway*.

"My granddaughter Elsie loves your show," a woman who told me to call her Mildred informs me as Harriet shepherds us across a street. "She lives with me and we've been watching it together. I can't tell you how pleased I am that your sister is such a good example to these young girls." She shakes her head. "I would get so tired of some of the trashy shows that Elsie used to watch. Shopping with her used to be a nightmare. It seemed the poor girl was determined to look like a call girl." She chuckles as we get in line again. "Although I have to admit Paige's influence comes at a price."

"What do you mean?" Suddenly I'm worried that Mildred has already seen the latest tabloids.

"Now Elsie wants expensive designer clothes. I finally had to put her on a budget before she drags me to the poor house." She laughs. "But I must say I'd rather spend money on those nice clothes then the horrid rags poor Elsie used to wear. That is an improvement."

The line is moving again and I put my focus on the words of our tour guide and the charming buildings. After we've seen the home of Shakespeare's birth and Nash's, the place where he died in 1616, we visit Hall's Croft, the house where his daughter and her wealthy husband lived. It has a lovely photogenic garden where I get a number of good photos. Then we visit Holy Trinity Church, and finally get on the bus and continue on to the cottage of Anne Hathaway, Shakespeare's wife.

By the time we finish it's not even one and I'm wondering how this can be an all-day tour, but to my surprise Stratford-upon-Avon is just the beginning. We also stop in Oxford where I take a full card's worth of photos, and then we stop at Windsor Castle, which is perfectly lit by a gorgeous dusky sky, translating into another card's worth of photos. Finally we return to London around eight and I tell all my new teacher friends good-bye. Okay, it wasn't exactly the kind of day I would brag about to anyone my age—I mean, hanging with a bunch of retired teachers probably sounds pretty lame. But I actually had a good time. I feel like I experienced more of England than I thought would be possible on this trip.

Of course, as I go into the hotel, which is thankfully free of paparazzi, I am exhausted. I'm barely in my room and am just getting ready for bed when Paige comes rushing through the adjoining door and falls onto my bed, sobbing.

"What's wrong?" I ask in horror as I pop my head out of my nightgown.

"Everything," she cries.

"What?" I demand, sitting down next to her. "Is it Mom?"

She sits up and looks at me with a tear-streaked face. "Where have you been all day?"

"On a bus tour—but tell me, is it Mom? Did something happen?"

"No ... it's not Mom. Mom is fine, although she was a bit miffed at you. She'd tried to call you—and so did I—but it seems your phone was turned off."

I shrug. "I didn't see any reason to leave it on."

"Well, except for the fact that you are here with me and here with our show and I was in the midst of a crisis!"

"What crisis?" I demand. I look closely at her now. "I don't see any broken bones, no bleeding wounds. What are you talking about?"

"I had the worst day ever."

"And ...?" Okay, I hate to seem totally unfeeling, but what am I supposed to do about it?

"And it would've been nice to have had you around ... for moral support, you know?"

"But all you wanted to do was sleep in and do a little

shopping," I remind her. "I can hardly see how you'd need my help to do that."

"Except for the paparazzi."

"You had paparazzi following you while you were shopping?"

She nods. "They were horrible. And being by myself—well, they just kept hammering away at me. They all seem certain that Ben and I are going to be married, that I'm pregnant, that Ben is a dirty rat, as they called him. It's all getting bigger and bigger." She sighs. "It's like the blogs' and networks' stories have taken on a life of their own and no matter what I say or do, no one is listening."

"Welcome to celebrity." I hold up my hands in a helpless gesture. "I mean … what did you expect, Paige?"

"A little more respect."

"Are you serious?" I study her and wonder if she's really as naïve about this as she sounds. "You used to follow all the tabloids and Hollywood gossip yourself," I remind her. "Remember how obsessed you were when Brad Pitt dumped Jennifer for Angelina? You totally hated Angelina for almost a year."

"Well, I was young and silly."

"And you were reading the tabloids and believing everything you read, Paige. Exactly what some people are doing right now."

"But how do I stop them?"

I shrug. "I have no idea. How did Angelina get you to stop believing that she was the devil and had destroyed Jennifer Aniston's life?"

She makes a sheepish smile. "I'm not sure she has stopped me."

"Oh, Paige." I shake my head.

"I'm kidding." She lets out a long sigh.

"It's the price of fame," I tell her. "You know what they say — if you can't take the heat ..."

"But it's so unfair ... and mean." She looks at me. "I would think you, of all people, would see how wrong it is. I would think you would be outraged, Erin."

"I'll admit that it really aggravates me. When I'm with you, I'll try to speak out, like I've been doing. But I don't think we can really stop them. Short of a lawsuit, and I'm not sure that even works."

"What were you doing today?"

So I tell her about my bus tour with a bunch of old schoolteachers, and she actually looks envious. "That sounds like fun."

I can't help but laugh. I mean, seriously, go figure!

Chapter 15

As exhausted as I was, once Paige got done unloading on me I was wide awake. Now I can't sleep. Something about this whole thing gets me. So I take out my computer and begin to write. My goal is to just get some of these thoughts down, at least for now. Maybe someday I'll do like Helen has suggested and start my own blog. Or not.

Other than snickering over the occasional sensational headline while waiting in a checkout line, I've never paid much attention to tabloids and gossip rags. Mollie used to buy them sometimes, until she discovered she could find her dirt for free online. But I've always kind of stayed away from the smut. It never interested me before . . . and it wouldn't interest me now except that suddenly it's feeling personal.

Being in London has really opened up my eyes about this business. I've concluded that, although tabloids cover—and oftentimes create—a variety of stories (including bizarre alien abductions and UFO sightings), they seem to favor one particular sort of "breaking news event."

And that is anything that involves the public humiliation

of a popular celebrity. Of course, if the person weren't a celebrity—a person of interest—there would be no point in public humiliation. Because everyone knows that writing embarrassing stories about ordinary people will not sell newspapers.

I've decided that tabloids thrive on celebrity downfall—or anything that can be portrayed as downfall. Their list of favorite topics include divorce, arrest, unwed pregnancy, bad parenting, rehab treatment, weight gain, arrests, or any negative experience that a public figure might prefer to keep private. And, naturally, the bigger the celebrity, the bigger the story.

But it seems to me that it wasn't until this London trip that Paige became such a big focus of this mean-spirited mudslinging. Why is London so interested in tearing my sister to shreds in their tabloid papers? To answer that question, I go to the lowest common denominator—money. Of course, those papers are all about making money. If consumers didn't buy those smutty tabloids, they wouldn't get printed. So apparently, there are people out there who enjoy reading bad things about my sister.

Again, I have to ask myself *why?* Why does the average person enjoy reading unkind and often untrue stories about a celeb? What makes men and women plunk down their hard-earned money to read what are mostly lies about someone they don't even know?

After much deliberation, I have come to the conclusion that some people are just plain jealous and as a result they're willing to buy into gossip and slander to make themselves feel better.

And so, even though I still think misleading tabloids are wrong-wrong-wrong, I guess I get why they're so popular. It's a human way of compensating. Some might go as far as to say this is how the playing field gets evened—a chance for the haves and the have-nots to be equal. The secret cost of fame, and a way celebrities pay their dues for being idolized, is by being victimized by tabloids. Blah, blah, blah ... finally I even put myself to sleep.

Of course, morning comes and I have to shove my philosophical and slightly judgmental musings aside and get ready to "perform" with my star sister. The irony of this does not escape me. Fortunately, and probably because it's early, we manage to exit the hotel without any fanfare.

"Where do you think they went?" Paige asks as the car pulls away.

"You sound like you miss them," I point out.

"No," she says quickly. "It's more like noticing that a toothache stopped."

"Well, I spoke to hotel security," Fran says. "They promised to do what they can, but they also reminded me that there are other fashion personalities staying at the hotel who appreciate being pursued by paparazzi."

Our first appointment is with Vivienne Westwood, the designer responsible for bringing punk into the mainstream, and I can't believe how easily Paige converses with this woman who must be almost fifty years her senior. Of course, I have to give much of that credit to Ms. Westwood, who seems like she's about our age and masquerading as an older woman.

"You are what I would call an extreme designer," Paige says finally. "Years ago you were instrumental in the punk trend in fashion and most recently your designs were featured in the movie *Sex and the City*." Paige smiles as if remembering. "I must say that wedding gown was exquisite and I wasn't a bit surprised when Carrie picked it to wear in her wedding."

Then Paige wraps up this interview and we head on to the next appointment, which amazingly enough is with former supermodel Naomi Campbell. Paige is ecstatic because she believes Naomi is one of the most beautiful women in the world. But when we get there, it seems that Naomi has changed her mind and her assistant informs us that Naomi only wants to do a one-on-one interview with Paige and one camera guy. Naturally, Paige agrees. Paige and JJ remain behind while Fran, the rest of the crew, and I go out for coffee.

"What was up with that?" I ask Fran as we sip our java and kill time.

"I'm guessing that Naomi wanted to be sure she had control of the interview."

"Why?"

"She's experienced some publicity issues."

"As in bad publicity?"

Fran nods.

"So does she think we're going to give her bad publicity?"

"I hear it's happened. Frankly, I was surprised that Leah was able to line up the interview in the first place." She frowns and looks at her watch. "I just hope it's going okay."

"Meaning what? How could it not go okay?"

"Hopefully Paige won't ask any incendiary questions."

"Such as?"

Fran rolls her eyes. "Such as some alleged assaults."

"You mean Naomi's been assaulted?"

"I mean Naomi's been accused of assaulting others."

"Oh ... well, hopefully she and Paige won't start smacking each other around." I laugh to imagine my sister putting up her fists against anyone—especially someone as gorgeous as Naomi Campbell.

Fran laughs. "Yes, I suppose that's unlikely."

And when we go back to pick up Paige, she seems completely pleased with her interview, telling us that Naomi Campbell couldn't be nicer. "She even does some great charity work with children in sub-Saharan Africa," Paige tells us as we drive back to our hotel for a little break.

"So why was she so worried about having the crew at the interview?" I ask.

"She's seen some of the bad publicity I've been getting," Paige admits. "She thought I might be out for revenge in my own interviews."

"Do people even do that?" I ask.

Paige shrugs. "I guess so."

Fortunately, we are able to get into our hotel without any unwanted fanfare. Then we meet with the crew in Paige's suite to look over tomorrow's appointments, making some game plans. While we're meeting, a room service lunch that Fran previously arranged for is delivered.

"What is this?" Alistair asks as he picks at a veggie platter. "Model food?"

Fran laughs. "Maybe so."

"Where do we go to get some real food?" JJ teases.

"Or is this a hint?" Shauna shakes a celery stick at Fran. "Are you saying we need to lose some weight?"

"No," Fran tells her. "I just ordered from the menu. I can't help it if they cater more to anorexics. Consider their usual clientele."

"Speaking of anorexics," I glance at tomorrow's schedule. "Kate Moss is our first appointment." I look at Paige. "I don't want to point fingers, but some people have. Are you going to ask her about her eating habits?"

Paige laughs then shakes her head. "No way."

"Why not?" I demand.

"Because that's not the point of my interview."

"Why isn't it?"

Paige looks at Fran, but Fran just shrugs.

"I was promised a show about body image and eating disorders," I remind both of them. "Kate Moss would be a great place to start. Do you realize that she started the waif look?"

"That's a matter of opinion." Paige picks up a carrot stick.

"Hey, maybe I should get the camera out," JJ suggests. He's already on his feet, going for his bag.

"Not a bad idea," Fran says. "Are you girls okay with that? Taping your candid conversation about this subject?" She points to me. "We could use this in your segment, Erin."

And so we agree. The next thing I know Paige and I are seated on the swanky sofa in her suite, going head-to-head about models and how they influence the average American woman.

"So are you telling me that you think Kate Moss had nothing to do with the stick-thin model craze that took hold during the nineties, or that her influence on fashion hasn't impacted the way the average American teen girl views her body?"

"That's a lot to pin on one person," Paige counters. "I don't see how you can blame Kate Moss for every eating disorder in America."

"I'm not trying to blame Kate Moss personally," I point out. "After all, it was the fashion industry that hired Kate to model in the first place. The industry helped to make her a star. She was pretty young so maybe she couldn't help that she was skinny. She probably had no way of knowing what a health hazard she would become to the average American woman."

Paige laughs. "Health hazard? Don't you think that's blowing it a bit out of proportion, Erin?"

"No, I don't. Not only was her lifestyle of under-eating a bad example, she may have used drugs too."

"Allegedly."

"Where there's smoke there's fire," I say and then wish I hadn't. "What I mean is that a lot of models use drugs to stay thin. Cocaine, amphetamines. It's no secret, Paige. Let's not pretend it doesn't exist. Okay?"

She shrugs. "Okay. What's your point?"

"My point is that Kate Moss is a huge influence in the fashion industry. I would think she could take some responsibility for that influence. Like it or not, she's a role model in the industry for young women. She needs to own up to some things and help others make better choices."

"Why?" Paige frowns. "Why should Kate Moss suddenly take responsibility for the choices we make? She's a fashion model—not a life counselor."

"Think about the word *model*," I say suddenly. "What does it mean?"

Paige actually looks stumped.

"Model, just by nature of the word, means something we look to as an example. Or it can be an imitation. It can even be an ideal. So women who work as fashion models should know that they are examples. Examples that others will want to imitate and that they might even be perceived as an ideal."

"But they're simply modeling the clothes."

"You can say that, Paige, but I know you don't believe it. Even you follow the personal lives of some of your favorite models. And someone like Kate Moss, who is still in the spotlight, has followers too. Women, especially young ones, want to look like her. Even to the point were some will resort to bad choices like eating disorders and drugs to accomplish it."

Paige seems to be considering this. "But models have always been thin, Erin. Everyone knows clothes look better on thin models."

"That's not true. I did some research and both actresses and models used to weigh more. Yes, there were a couple of short eras when the stick-thin models were popular for a while. But for the most part, models have been tall and slender, but not anorexic—at least they didn't *look* that way. Before Kate Moss's influence, the most popular models were women like Cindy Crawford, Claudia Schiffer, and Naomi Campbell."

Paige nods. "I can see you've done some research."

"I have. What I want to know is why we can't get back to that. Why can't we accept that the female human body is supposed to have curves, or that women are meant to carry more body fat than men, or that starving yourself or taking drugs to lose weight is a big mistake?"

Paige sighs. "Good points."

We continue sparring for a while longer, and finally I get Paige to agree to bring up this subject with Kate Moss tomorrow. "I'll put it in a non-confrontational way," she says as if thinking out loud. "I'll ask Kate to speak a bit about body image and health . . . and what kind of influence she thinks the fashion world in general has on women. That shouldn't be too intimidating." Paige looks at me. "Will that make you happy?"

I smile. "It's a start."

"And that's a wrap," Fran says. "Now we need to get ready for our last appointment of the day."

I feel like I gained a bit of ground this afternoon. Okay, maybe it's only a tiny bit of ground, and it remains to be seen whether or not my sister will be true to her word tomorrow. But I've decided that if she just happens to forget her little resolve to ask Kate her non-confrontational question ... well, I might have to help her out a bit. After all, I am supposed to be costarring in this show.

Chapter
16

Our next appointment is with Jenny Pack-ham, a popular Brit designer. To our surprise, she actually has set up a mini fashion show for us. I have to say her evening gowns are stunning. She uses a lot of beads and adornments along with interesting fabrics, and the end result is truly beautiful. My only complaint, which I keep to myself, is that her models—while pretty—look a little hungry. I wished I'd thought ahead to sneak some pastries into the changing area, although I'm sure I would've been raked over the coals for such a subversive attempt.

"Wasn't that fantastic?" Paige says as we're riding back through London. "I don't know when I've seen such gorgeous gowns. You could take me to her showroom, blindfold me, and let me pick out any one of them and I'd be happy."

"That's high praise. But I have to admit Jenny's designs were magical," I say. "She reminds me a little of our designer friend Rhiannon, in New York, although Jenny's designs are more sophisticated."

"I can't wait to see her wedding dress collection," Paige says. "That show is on Saturday."

"So what do you girls think?" Fran says. "Want to eat out or go back to the hotel for room service?"

Remembering our "model" lunch, I opt for going out and, thankfully, Paige agrees. As we drive Fran calls ahead and finds a popular place in Soho where the wait will only be fifteen minutes.

"Do you think any paparazzi will be around?" Paige asks quietly.

"I don't see why," Fran tells her. "Unless you're sending information onto one of the social networks."

"Of course not." Paige firmly shakes her head. "And I spoke to Benjamin last night—told him that he'd better not do anything else to fuel this fire."

"Has he?" I ask.

She shrugs. "He hasn't helped to put any rumors to rest."

"I'm sure he's enjoying the free publicity," Fran says.

"Free at my expense, you mean."

When we're dropped at the restaurant, we go in without any sign of paparazzi. I do notice a few heads turn as we're being seated, but I remind myself that's always been how it is with Paige. She turns heads and she enjoys doing so.

"Maybe the paparazzi have found bigger stories to follow," Paige says as we're browsing our menus.

"You sound like you miss them," I point out.

She shrugs. "No. But no one wants to be ignored either."

I can't help but laugh at how flaky that sounds. "I don't mind being ignored," I tell her. "At least by paparazzi anyway."

We eat our dinner in peace and quiet and exit the restaurant with no unwanted fanfare. Unwanted from me that is … I'm not so sure about Paige. But when we get back to our hotel, there seems to be a fair number of people clustered around the entrance again.

"Oh no," Paige says in alarm. "I guess our little reprieve is over."

"Want me to go ahead?" I offer, "and act as a smokescreen so you can slip in the side door?"

She seems uncertain, but Fran agrees to this plan. When I get to the door, however, I see that the spotlight is shining for someone else. It turns out that Tyra Banks and her entourage have just arrived. It seems they're here for the taping of her show and the upcoming fashion events next week. I laugh to myself as I go back to inform my sister that she is no longer the hottest fashion story in London.

Paige seems disappointed as she gets out of the car, and strides toward the entrance of the hotel like she's a superstar. Seriously, she's like *look at me, I'm so hot. Don't you want a shot of me?*

And to my dismay her persona works. It seems that Tyra and her crew have gone inside now, and since the paparazzi are already gathered, they turn their cameras onto Paige. Just as I expected, these "journalists" show how small-minded they are since their questioning goes straight to the Benjamin Kross relationship again: is Paige pregnant and when is the big wedding?

"Really," she says in a tone that might be interpreted as haughty. "Can't you come up with anything better than that? Why don't you write a story about how a flying saucer full of fashion-conscious aliens from Venus brought me here so that I could spy out fashion trends on Earth and—"

"Why are you always avoiding the questions?" a guy interrupts her. "There's no crime in being in love with a man — even if he has broken the law. In this day and age, it's not a big deal to be pregnant when you're not married, Paige. People do it all the time. Just own up to it and we'll let you be."

"That's right," yells another, "own up to it and we'll be on our merry way."

"All we want is the truth," a woman calls out.

"The truth?" she shouts at them. "You want the truth?"

No one responds. It's as if they're waiting for some choice morsel of gossip.

"The truth is I'm sick of you Brits posting bogus photos and printing lies about me. I don't know how you can look at yourselves in the mirror when you get up in the morning. If you keep this up I will be speaking to my attorney." She turns around and nearly stumbles over the woman standing behind her. I grab Paige's arm, steadying her, and the two of us push our way through the grumbling throng, who apparently didn't appreciate Paige's comments. We find Fran standing in the lobby with an I-told-you-so look on her face.

"Happy now?" Fran asks her.

Paige smiles. "As a matter of fact, I am."

However, she is singing another song the next morning. "Look at how they're maligning me now," she says as we're standing in the lobby, waiting for our car to arrive and take us to our Kate Moss interview.

"Where did you get that?" I frown as I spot one of Britain's most popular tabloids in her hand.

"Here in the gift shop." She thrusts the paper at me. "This morning's edition. Look what they said about me."

As Fran joins us, I scan the headline — "Paige Forrester

Blasts Britain." For Fran's sake, I read the words out loud. "'Miss Forrester, star of America's *On the Runway*, in an angry outburst against Great Britain said, "The truth is I'm sick of you Brits, and I don't know how you can look at yourselves in the mirror." Apparently Miss Forrester, a self-proclaimed fashion diva, is under the impression that no one in Great Britain has any fashion sense whatsoever, and it seems that she plans to make this clear on her reality TV show. Miss Forrester went on to say that she planned to seek legal counsel to sue any paper who printed her statement. Miss Forrester is a guest in Great Britain, with plans to make an appearance on our popular reality show, *Britain's Got Style*, but the question on many a Brit's mind this morning is whether or not Miss Forrester has any style herself. Not to mention class. Miss Forrester is reputed to be pregnant with—'"

"*Stop!*" Paige rips the paper from my hands. "I can't take another word!"

"Oh, dear." Fran shakes her head. "This is not good."

"How can they print such lies?"

"I don't know," Fran says in a grim tone. "But the car is here. Let's go."

I take the rumpled paper back from Paige and as we're riding, I reread the opening sentence of the article again—silently this time. "Actually, it's not all lies," I say quietly.

"Not lies?" Paige looks like she's on the verge of tears now. "How can you, my very own sister, say that?"

"Because it's true. I was with you last night and I heard you talking." I point to the paper. "You *did* say you were sick of the Brits, Paige. You also said you didn't know how they could look at themselves in the mirror. Maybe you didn't mean it in the context that they took it, but you did say those words."

Paige lets out a low animal-like growl. "They twisted it, Erin. You know they did."

"They twisted your meaning to make a story," I tell her. "But you did say those words."

"Quiet," Fran tells us. "I can't hear this message."

So we both sit quietly as Fran listens to her voicemail with a severe frown.

"Who is it?" Paige asks.

"Kate Moss's spokesperson."

"And?" I wait.

"Kate has cancelled this morning's interview and has no intention of rescheduling."

Paige makes two tight-balled fists. "Why?"

"Sounds like she's been following the press and she doesn't want to be linked with you."

"This is so unfair!" Paige slumps back into the seat, her head hanging.

"It is unfair," I admit. "But you opened yourself up for it again when you spoke to the paparazzi last night. You could've easily slipped past them, you know."

"Please. Do. Not. Lecture. Me." Paige looks like she's about ready to blow and so I decide to be quiet as Fran tells the driver to take us back to the hotel. Fortunately, it must be too early for the paparazzi because the entrance is still pretty empty. We all quietly go inside and without anyone saying a word, we ride back up the elevator and walk into our rooms.

So now I'm pacing in my room, and thinking, *this is great. Just great.* We're over here to record episodes and suddenly, because Paige has stuck her foot in her mouth, it looks like we're being shut down almost before we're even started. Seriously, if Kate Moss doesn't want to talk to us, why would anyone else? And why would *Britain's Got Style* still want Paige on their show?

It's like Paige got off on the wrong foot with this country as soon as we got here. I can't really blame her for anything specific in regard to the paparazzi — well, before last night anyway. At first she was actually polite to the rabid reporters. But I can blame her for blabbing on the social networks and for tweeting before we even got here. I can also blame her for her indiscretion with Benjamin. I never thought that was a good idea. Benjamin has always had a bad-boy image with the press and with Mia Renwick's death, his image has only gotten worse. I'm frankly surprised that he still has a movie offer — if that's even true.

"Erin?" Paige sticks her head through the open door between her suite and my room.

"What?"

"I need to talk."

Okay, I'm not sure I'm ready to talk to her yet. The fact is I'm feeling a little mad at the moment. When I think of how I've sacrificed most of my first year of film school to get to this point ... well, it's a little disturbing.

"Will you come in here?" she asks.

Without answering, I follow her back into her suite then collapse on the sofa and let out a big deep sigh.

"I don't know what to do," she says quietly. "Fran is mad at me, which means Helen is mad at me." She looks up with moist blue eyes. "Are you mad at me too?"

I just frown.

"Okay, I'll take that as a yes."

I fold my arms across my front and sit there.

"I don't know what to do ..." she says again.

"I don't either."

"But you're the one who usually has the answers," she tells me.

"I'm fresh out at the moment, Paige."

So we both sit there in silence. While I'm sure I could think of something if I tried hard enough, I'm just not willing to try. I'd rather let her stew in this mess she's helped cook up. Savor the flavor. I keep sitting there, simply looking down at my lap, until finally I glance up, to see that she's gone.

So much for coming up with solutions. I'm about to return to my room when I hear the sounds coming from her bedroom. I go in there to find her stretched out on the bed, quietly crying. Something about this gets to me. Maybe it's because she's not being a drama queen. This is real.

I sit down beside her and wait for her to stop. But the crying goes on for quite some time and I finally reach over and touch her hair. "Crying isn't going to fix this," I say quietly. "When you're ready to listen, I think I have some ideas."

She keeps on crying and now I don't know what to do. I mean, I know my sister and I know she can overreact and get wildly emotional sometimes, but this seems like honest-to-goodness despair. So I go over to Fran's room and explain what's going on.

"I suppose I was kind of hard on her after we got up here," Fran admits. "But Paige knows that a lot rides on her. Helen has made it clear that she expects Paige to keep a relatively clean reputation. Our sponsors expect it too."

"But most of the stuff that's being printed about her isn't even true," I remind Fran.

"Perception can be stronger than truth." Fran shakes her

head. "Now I'm finding out that Kate Moss isn't the only one to cancel on Paige."

"Oh …" I let out a sigh. "I was worried about that."

"British people don't take kindly to being insulted by a twenty-year-old fashion diva."

"No, I expect they don't."

"Anyway, I'm glad you came over to talk. Helen has a new plan." She waves me to a chair to sit down. "She thinks that her little Jiminy Cricket might be able to save this sinking ship."

"How?"

"First of all, both you and Paige will hold a press conference. Helen wants a repentant Paige to stay in the background while you step up and make a very sincere and intelligent apology. Do you think you can do that?"

"I guess so."

"Helen said it's important that you don't make this an attempt to clean up your sister's smeared reputation. Just let that go for now. Mostly you have the challenging task of winning back the Brits." She actually laughs. "Now that sounds easy, doesn't it?"

"Right." I roll my eyes. "Easy breezy."

"Okay. I'll set up the press conference." She looks at my outfit. "You change into something that looks British and slightly serious." She chuckles. "Kind of like your usual clothing."

"I happen to really like British style," I admit.

"Make that work for you."

I stand now. "So that's it."

"That's it for now. I'll admit it's a long shot … but it's worth a try."

"Do you want me to tell Paige?"

She nods as she picks up her phone. "Sure. I'd appreciate that."

I go back to Paige's suite and attempt to tell her about Helen's plan, but I'm not sure she's getting it. She still seems to be a basket case. So, once again, I sit on the edge of her bed. "Paige," I say gently. "Is there more going on here than this bad publicity?"

She sits up now, wiping her wet face with her hands. "What do you mean?"

"It just seems like an overreaction. I mean, we've been through some really difficult stuff before. It seems like you're taking this especially hard. What's really going on?"

Paige takes in a long breath. "I miss Dylan."

I blink and stare at her. "Huh?"

"I know. It sounds really dumb. But I think I'm in love with him."

I want to agree—this does sound really dumb, especially right now—but I control myself. "I don't get it. What do you mean you miss him . . . that you think you're in love with him? I thought you guys broke it off. That you were going to just be friends. Did I miss something?" She nods and now fresh tears are coming down her cheeks. And, okay, I'm totally bewildered. Like how is this breakdown about Dylan? But she's crying so hard again that I doubt I can get to the bottom of it. I'm not even sure I want to.

Chapter
17

"*First of all, I want to apologize on behalf of* my sister and myself," I say after Fran introduces me at the press conference that's being held in one of the hotel conference rooms. The audience looks grim and although Paige and Fran are standing nearby, I feel very much on my own. It's some comfort to spot our camera guys in the back of the room, acting like they're part of the press.

"Yesterday, my sister made a statement that was misconstrued." I glance at my notes—notes that Fran read and approved. "Paige spoke out in frustration last night. Her comments were in reference to a misrepresentation in some tabloids. She said she was sick of Brits, but not all Brits, only *Brits who had been printing false stories and bogus photos to smear her name.* But as for everyone else in Great Britain, we have nothing but the highest praise. We love your country." I break away from my notes now, hoping to make this seem more personal. "I enjoyed taking a bus tour of the countryside. I couldn't believe how beautiful it is here. And your amazing buildings and Windsor Castle—well, let's just say we don't have anything like that where I live." I pause for a few chuckles and hope that they're warming up a bit. "I've enjoyed the food and I had my first rashers. I've enjoyed meeting people and I love the way you guys talk. And I have to say—I adore British fashion." I smile at the faces, noticing that some seem softer now.

"There are so many things about your country that I love that I'm thinking maybe I'm actually British at heart." I pause for the laughs that follow. "But I mostly want you to understand that Paige was misquoted. I was there when she made the statement about not knowing how British tabloid reporters can look at themselves in the mirror in the morning. She wasn't talking about Brits and fashion." I shake my head. "She was simply referring to how a dishonest reporter might feel after writing an article that slandered Paige's name." I pause again. "I'm sure you can imagine how it feels to have someone reporting malicious and untrue things about you. It hurts. Paige's outburst was a result of the libelous things that have been said about her. But because we are guests in your country, we feel it's our responsibility to apologize and attempt to set the record straight. Thank you for your graciousness." I smile and nod, and as I step away from the podium I'm surprised to hear several people clapping. They are joined by more and I feel hopeful.

Fran steps back up to the podium again. "And Erin is happy to give honest answers to your questions now." As I step back up, Fran and Paige exit and I am left on my own with reporters. But for the most part, the questions are relatively polite and I do my best to answer them.

"No, my sister is not pregnant," I say slowly. "The photo you saw a couple days ago was taken when I was shopping with my best friend who happens to be pregnant. Then someone photoshopped the photo of me by a baby crib with a photo of Paige to give the impression she was pregnant."

"But what about her relationship with Benjamin Kross?" someone shouts from the back. "Are you saying those photos were tampered with too?"

I firmly shake my head. "No. Those photos are legit. Paige and Benjamin have dated in the past." I pause now, wondering how much to say. "Okay, I'm going to be very honest with you and I hope my sister doesn't get mad." I take in a slow breath and I can tell the reporters are eagerly waiting. "Paige just confessed to me that the main reason this whole thing has been so stressful is because she is, in fact, in love with someone. But it's not Benjamin Kross." Okay, even as I speak, I'm wondering if I just made a huge mistake. Of course, I have no intention of revealing who that someone else is. Naturally a whole new set of questions follow and now everyone wants to know about the mystery guy.

"All I can say is that it's not Benjamin Kross," I say with an air of finality, like this interview is over. "Paige was only spending time with Benjamin as a friend. I can't speak for his interest in my sister, but take it from me Paige Forrester is not romantically interested in Benjamin Kross."

"How about you?" someone calls out. "How's the little sister's love life?"

I laugh. "Well, I've got several guy friends, but I'm not ready for anything serious."

Fortunately the rest of the questions are fairly innocuous and mostly in regard to the show. As the crowd dwindles and interest fades, I thank them for their time, remove the microphone, and excuse myself.

"Why did you tell them that?" Paige demands when I join her and Fran in a little side room where they've been sitting and listening to all that I said. I can tell she's nervous, and probably more scared than she'll admit.

"I wanted to lead them off the Benjamin trail," I tell her.

"That's a good idea," Fran agrees. "It's okay to stir some curiosity about Paige's love life. After all, we don't want to cut the press loose from us. Publicity is publicity."

Paige sighs with a sad expression. "I guess."

"I told Paige that she's going to take the rest of the day off," Fran tells me.

"What about our interviews?"

"They're fairly small ones." Fran smiles at me. "I think you can handle them."

"Alone?"

Fran nods. "You just handled the London press alone. Surely you can handle a couple of small-potato interviews."

"I appreciate it, Erin." Paige makes a weak smile. "I'll get it back together by tomorrow. I promise."

I study her and wonder what happens if she *can't* get it back together. But then I remind myself that she always gets it back together. She's the queen of bounce-back.

The first interview turns out to be just the sort of thing I really like. Ashley Amberly is only twenty-seven and a relatively new designer who is refreshingly green. She only uses fabrics made from renewable resources in her designs — like bamboo, wood fibers, hemp, recycled plastic, polyester, organic cotton, and linen. But she has a huge British following.

"Most of my customers are young people," she tells me as we're winding down. "So I try to keep my designs affordable.

Although I've been encouraged to create a couture line for next year's London Fashion Week. I'm thinking about it."

"What would be the advantage of participating in Fashion Week?" I ask her. "I mean, since you already have a solid consumer base of environmentally conscious customers."

She frowns as if thinking. "You know … that's a good question. On one hand, it's flattering to be invited to the ball, but on the other hand it might be offensive to some of my green groupies." She smiles. "Not to mention PETA."

"I know Stella McCartney is a strong supporter of animal rights."

Ashley nods vigorously. "I'm a huge fan of Stella McCartney."

"Have you heard of Granada Greenwear?"

"Oh, yes. Granada's been an inspiration too."

"Has anyone ever considered doing a Green Fashion Week?" I ask.

Ashley's eyes light up. "That is a brilliant idea, Erin."

"Thanks." I smile. "I know I'd want to attend it."

"If you don't mind, I might steal that idea and attempt to run with it."

"You're more than welcome. Just promise to keep me posted. Maybe *On the Runway* could participate with you."

We talk for a while longer and Ashley's enthusiasm is contagious. But finally Fran gives me the wrap-it-up sign and I thank Ashley for her time.

"That was great," Ashley tells me as we're removing our mics. "You do a fabulous interview, Erin. Your big sister better watch out."

"Thanks. But I don't think she has too much to worry about."

"Nice work," Fran tells me as we drive to the next appointment.

"Ashley was just my cup of tea," I admit. "That made it easy."

"The next one should be fairly straightforward too." She looks at her notes. "Gregory Maxwell is a popular British jewelry designer, but since he's in Thailand, his assistant Valerie will show us his studio."

"Do we know anything about his style?"

"Just that he's quite popular in the UK." Fran shrugs. "Let's wing it and hope that this Valerie is a talker."

Thankfully Valerie, who turns out to be Maxwell's daughter and not much older than me, is a talker, as well as an apprentice jewelry maker. And her dad's work turns out to be absolutely lovely. Again, I think I got lucky because his nature-inspired designs are just the kinds of things I like. He imitates the beauty of flowers, plants, birds, fish, and small animals, combining his graceful designs with precious and semi-precious gems to create some absolutely charming pieces.

"I love this," I say as I examine a silver vine-like necklace with seed pearls posing as pussy willows.

"Our designs are primarily sold in the UK, but we've also expanded into a number of international markets," Valerie tells us. "We've recently become rather well liked in Asia. My father's work became internationally known in the nineties when some of his pieces were worn by Kate Holloway."

So for the most part, and to my relief, Valerie plays both tour guide and narrator. Finally we're done and I'm thanking her.

"I must've seemed like such a chatterbox," she says as she

hands back her mic. "I was just so thrilled about this opportunity. I hope I didn't muck anything up for your show."

I smile. "No, you were perfect. We'll send you a DVD of the show when it airs. That way your father can see what a great job you did today."

It's nearly six by the time we get back to the hotel. As we're walking through the lobby, I'm surprised to see that I have a phone message on my iPhone. And even more surprised when I see it's from Dylan Marceau.

"I'm going to swing by the gift store," Fran tells me. "Need anything?"

"No. I'm fine." As she heads off, I find a quiet corner and I listen to the message.

"Erin, you're probably wondering why I'm calling you. A little British bird just told me something this morning … and I was hoping you could give me a quick call." Then he leaves his cell phone number and I glance around, worried that someone might be around to eavesdrop on my conversation if I return his call. But I seem to be the only one here. And if I go to my room to call, the connectivity is sketchy at best, plus Paige might walk in on me. I'm pretty sure this is going to be about her. I decide to just get this over with.

"Erin?" he says happily. "How are you?"

"Okay."

"I heard about your press conference."

"Seriously? Who told you?"

"A Brit fashion friend. But never mind that. I'd seen some of the other stories about Paige and Benjamin in the news lately … and I think it was very nice of you to help your sister out of that mess."

"Well, it was kind of turning into everyone's mess." I tell him about Kate Moss's cancellation.

"Maybe I could give Kate a call," he says. "She's an old friend."

"You seem to have a lot of friends."

He laughs. "Well, it's helpful in this business. I consider you a good friend too, Erin."

"Thanks, Dylan. Same back at you." I glance around again, but I still seem to be alone.

"So ... my friend told me you said that Paige is romantically interested in someone else ..." His voice trails off.

"Uh ... right."

"I don't want to twist your arm to tell me about this mystery guy. But I want you to know you can trust me. I really care about Paige. Even though she broke my heart in Paris, I still want the very best for her life and—"

"She broke up with you?"

There's a long pause. "Well, it's not a tale I want everyone to hear. No guy likes getting dumped. But since you're her sister ... I assumed this would be old news to you anyway."

"Let me get this straight. You're saying Paige dumped you?"

"That might be an overstatement. As I recall I saw the writing on the wall that night. But, being a guy with a fair amount of pride, I probably acted as if the breakup was mutual."

"But it wasn't mutual?" I'm trying to wrap my head around this.

"So what are you saying, Erin? Did Paige tell you a different version?"

I try to remember now. "Well, to start with she told me it

was mutual. Back when she and I agreed to give up any serious relationships with guys and just focus on the show."

"Yes, that's about what she said that evening ... or what I refer to in my mind as the last supper."

"But you're saying she broke up with you?"

Another long pause. "What do you know? What is Paige saying to you, Erin?"

I consider this. Upstairs my sister is pining away. She's missed a whole day of work ... she cried for more than an hour this morning ... she admitted that she misses Dylan, that she thinks she loves him. But what am I supposed to do about it?

"Who is this guy, Erin? You can trust me. I swear I won't breathe a word to anyone."

"Oh, Dylan ... maybe you should talk to Paige."

"Really?"

"Yes," I say eagerly. "You really, really should talk to Paige. In fact, I have a very strong feeling she'll be extremely glad to hear your voice."

"You really think so?"

"I know so. I just think this is something I need to stay out of, you know?"

"I understand."

"She's probably in her room right now. You might want to call the landline though, since our cell phone service is a little sketchy in the hotel."

"You're sure it's a good idea?"

"Pretty sure."

"Thanks, Erin."

"Sure. But maybe you shouldn't tell Paige you talked to me, okay? I don't want her to think I'm meddling."

"You got it. I'll just start out the conversation low-key. Like I'm just calling to say hey . . . and see where we go from there."

"Sounds good." Then I give him Paige's room number. But after I hang up, I wonder what I've done.

"Hey, you still down here?" Fran comes around the corner and takes me by surprise.

"Oh, yeah," I say quickly. "Just using the phone down here since it doesn't work that well in my room."

"Everything okay at home?" she asks as I walk with her to the elevators.

"Sure. Everything's fine."

"You really did a good job today, Erin," she says as she pushes the button to our floor.

"Thanks. It was actually kind of fun. But I'll be relieved to have Paige up and running again."

"Do you think she's going to snap out of it?" Fran looks at me curiously. "She seems to be in a quite a slump. I didn't know this publicity crud would get to her like this."

"I'm sure she'll be fine tomorrow." I give Fran a hopeful smile. "She's pretty resilient."

"I hope you're right. We've got several great appointments back-to-back tomorrow, starting first thing in the morning. And the opening fashion show is tomorrow evening. After that we're booked with style shows throughout the day Saturday clear into Sunday night. If Paige doesn't kick it into gear and if we miss out on these opportunities, we'll be short on material when we get home next week. And Helen will not be pleased."

"I don't think you need to worry about Paige," I tell her as we get out of the elevator.

"I hope you're right." She looks at her watch, then covers

a yawn. "I plan to order in my dinner tonight. I've already arranged for breakfast to be delivered to Paige's suite tomorrow. The plan is to meet there for hair and makeup by eight o'clock sharp."

"Gotcha." I make a mock solute then turn toward my room. As I unlock and open the door, I try to imagine Paige's surprise when Dylan calls her out of the blue. Will she be happy, or shocked? Or will she figure out that I've been involved and get mad for my interference? With nothing else to do, I shoot up a silent prayer and tiptoe into my room where I'm tempted to lean my head against the adjoining door. Instead, I grab up my iPod, slip in the earbuds and, crossing my fingers, fall backward onto my bed where I intend to crash until hunger takes over.

Chapter
18

"What a gorgeous day," Paige says cheerfully as I come into her room through the adjoining door. I'm still in my pajamas and barely awake. But in here, all the drapes are pulled open and bright morning light is pouring in. The hair and makeup people have also arrived, and are milling around.

"Uh-huh," I say sleepily.

"What is wrong with your hair?" Luis frowns at me.

"It's clean," I say sheepishly. "I washed it last night."

He shakes his head, pointing toward the kitchenette. "Go wet yourself down like a good girl. I'll bring you a towel."

I nod and pad into the kitchen, turn on the water, adjust the temperature, then stick my head under the flow. I know how much Luis hates it when I wash my hair at night. I wake up looking like a scarecrow and it takes him longer to style it. But I like showering at night. At least my hair is short so it dries quickly.

"Here you go." He drapes a towel around my soggy head, then leans over and whispers in my ear. "What or who do you think is responsible for our Little Miss Merry Sunshine this morning?"

I wrap the towel tighter then stand up with a grin. "The sunshine perhaps?"

He rolls his eyes. "If only the sunshine were capable of such miracles ... the whole planet would be deliriously happy most of the time."

"We have a busy morning," Paige chirps as Shauna works on her makeup. "By the way, Erin, Fran said you did great yesterday. Thanks for covering for me!"

"You're welcome." I stop by where some food is set up and help myself to a muffin and a yogurt, which I plan to munch on while Luis does my hair. "It was actually kind of fun. Where is Fran anyway?"

"Getting some decent coffee downstairs." Luis wraps the styling cape around my shoulders. "Shauna and I threatened to go on strike if we had to keep drinking the stuff that's in our rooms."

"I offered to make them some here," Paige says, "but Fran said we need to hurry and get ready. I laid out an outfit for you on my bed, Erin. Business casual for the day, and then we'll come back and switch into something more festive for the fashion show tonight."

"You seem extra happy this morning," I say a bit cautiously.

"Oh, I am." She turns to me with a sunshiny face. "I really, really am."

"Care to share with the class?" Luis teases as he aims the blow dryer at my head.

"Not yet." She gives him a catty smile. "But maybe in time."

Well, I have no doubt that her change in mood is thanks to Dylan. I can't say I'm not appreciative, but this sudden act of secrecy is an interesting twist. Although, I can't say that I blame her after all the questionable media coverage she's had lately. Even though I'm sure we can trust Luis and Shauna, loose lips might still sink ships. *On the Runway's* ship is barely back to floating again as it is.

"It's such a nice day," I say as Luis rubs some product into my hair, "I think I'll get a hop-on, hop-off pass."

"A what?" Paige asks.

"It's a day pass for the double-decker buses," I explain. "The concierge told me about it. If you get one, you can just hop onto a bus and ride for a while, then hop off when you reach your destination."

"That sounds fun," Paige says. "Why don't you get me one too?"

"Get you one what?" Fran asks as she comes into the room with a cardboard carrier full of coffees.

"A double-decker bus pass," Paige tells her.

Then I explain the on and off concept. "I thought if we had a break or two today, which looks possible according to the schedule I studied last night, it might be fun to play tourist today. Especially since the sun is shining."

"I asked Erin to get me one too," Paige tells her.

"Really?" Fran looks surprised, and I am too. Because this does not sound like Paige to me.

"I plan to ride on top of the bus," I warn Paige, "out in the open air so I can really see things. You sure you want to do that?"

"Yeah. Why not?"

"You girls better take a scarf for your hair," Luis warns us.

"Oh, we can do touch-ups before each event," Shauna tells him. "Let the girls have some fun."

"Maybe we should send a camera along too," Fran says. "That would be a fun snippet to have on the London shows. I think I'll call down and get us several passes. This sounds like a great idea, Erin."

Now I'm feeling even more enthused. "I already checked the bus route map," I tell her. "It runs right through some of the areas we'll be in today. So I think it's doable."

"And tomorrow, before the first fashion show, we should get some shots of you girls in front of Buckingham Palace ... some flirting with the Beefeaters."

"What's a beef eater?" Paige asks as Shauna removes the makeup bib and gives it a shake.

"The guards in front of the palace," Fran tells her. "The ones with the tall furry hats."

"Actually, that's not quite right," I correct her. "The Beef-eaters guard the Tower of London."

"How do you know that?" Fran questions.

"I learned it on my tour the other day. A lot of people mistake the palace guards for Beefeaters, but that's not accurate. Although the palace guards do wear those tall bearskin hats."

"So what's up with the hats?" Paige comes over to wait for Luis to finish up on me.

Luis gives a final misting of spray to my hair. "There, maybe that will stand up to riding around on top of busses."

I stand up and let Paige take my place. "The tall hats were designed to make the soldiers look taller for battle. More intimidating."

"Ah-hah," Paige says. "You see, there are many reasons for various fashion statements."

Paige's sweet spirits continue on throughout the morning. She is gracious and kind to everyone — from the doormen to the CEOs. Her compliments flow like a river and yet each one sounds genuine and unique. Whether designers, models, or assistants, they all just warm right up to her aura of happiness. Every interview seems to go as smooth as butter. Really, it's like she can't say or do anything wrong. It appears the magic is back and everyone seems to adore her.

And, naturally, I am getting suspicious. What exactly did Dylan say to her last night? What could he have possibly done to bring about this miraculous transformation?

When we hop onto the double-decker bus, Paige is still full of sunshine and joy. Her mood is contagious as other tourists begin to laugh and joke with her, and she even manages to snag some interesting conversations which JJ catches on camera. Meanwhile I enjoy the London scenery, take a few photos myself, and actually listen as the guide explains what it is we're seeing.

Finally, the hardest part of our shooting for the day seems to be done, and after one more hop-on, hop-off bus ride we're back at the hotel with enough time to relax for a couple of hours before tonight's fashion show.

"I know," Paige says as we're riding up in the elevator. "Let's eat downstairs in the hotel restaurant tonight. We can dress up for the fashion show and then we'll walk into the restaurant and see how many heads we can turn. Jenny Packham was supposed to send over some dresses today."

I'm considering this. The truth is it's been a long day, and because this place is already crawling with models, I'm sure heads will be turning in every direction—not just at Paige.

"Come on," she urges me, "it'll be fun."

"Count me in," Fran tells her. "I'm willing and hungry."

"Erin?" She looks hopefully at me.

"Sure. I'm in."

"I'll call down for a reservation," Fran says as we're going into our rooms. "Let's say six. That should give us time to get to the show."

"Come on into my room," Paige calls to me. "I'll help with your hair and makeup and then we'll pick out a sizzling outfit."

It takes less than an hour until Paige and I are both dressed to the nines. As promised, Jenny Packham came through and sent over several fantastic-looking cocktail dresses. "Are you sure this isn't too much?" I ask Paige as I check out my image in the mirror. My dress is a black and hot pink number that reminds me a little of the Roaring Twenties with its beaded fringe and beautiful corset belt. Paige looks elegant in a silky dress of peacock blue with touches of beading around the neck and the waist. We're both wearing dark hose with a bit of sparkle to it — compliments of Jenny — and some very cool platform shoes.

"I feel like a grandma with you two," Fran says when she meets us in the suite. She has on a two-piece black dress that is actually quite nice.

"You look great," Paige tells her. "Sophisticated chic."

"Or middle-aged frump?"

"No way," Paige assures her. "You are hot, Fran."

I nod. "You always look great. Very director-like ... with authority and class."

She smiles. "Well, no one will be looking at me tonight anyway. You girls look stunning."

I suppose I was wrong about not turning any heads tonight. As we walk across the lobby, I notice a number of people looking. Some seem to know who we are, while others look curious. But everyone is rather nonchalant too, like no one wants to be caught looking.

We enjoy a nice dinner and as we're finishing up, I tell Paige thanks for coming up with a good idea. "This really was fun. Much better than eating in our rooms."

"See, you just need to trust me sometimes."

"I must commend you on your amazing comeback today," Fran tells her as she sips her coffee. "I already left a message for Helen telling her what a brilliant job you did today. Both you girls."

I shrug. "I didn't really do much."

"But I am curious, Paige. What made you able to pull yourself out of the depths like that? What's your secret tonic? Is it something we can bottle? Legal, I hope."

Paige just laughs.

"Maybe it was the sunshine," I say quickly. "It really was a pretty day."

"Yes," Paige agrees. "The sun came out and that makes everyone happy."

Fran looks a bit skeptical. But then she glances at her watch. "I better tell the driver to bring the car around if we want to get there in time to film some of the behind-the-scenes stuff. I'll bet the crew is already there."

"Do we need to check our hair or makeup?" I ask.

"No, you both look great."

"We'll touch up our lips in the car," Paige says.

As Paige and I are doing our last-minute primping, Fran's iPhone chimes. She lets out a little groan when she checks to see who's calling. "Hello, Mark," she says in a falsely cheery tone. "What's up?" As she listens, two sharp frown lines crease her forehead, and I can tell something is wrong.

"What happened?" I ask as she slides her phone back into her bag with a low growl.

"That was Mark McCall." She presses her lips together and folds her arms across her chest.

"The producer of *Britain's Got Style*?" Paige asks with a worried look.

Fran nods grimly. "He called to inform me that your presence is no longer needed on their show."

Paige's shoulders droop and she looks down into her lap. "Because of me."

"Or because Mark McCall is a great big chicken."

"I just don't get it," I declare. "I thought reality shows loved controversy and any kind of publicity. Mark should be grateful for all the press Paige has gotten recently. Viewership should be higher than—"

"Unfortunately, there seems to be a lot of pride involved here," Fran says crisply. "Maybe it's the old Brits-versus-Yanks competition, or maybe it's something more. I don't know. But I'm not eager to report to Helen."

"Is there anything I can do?" Paige asks meekly.

Fran lets out a long sigh. "Just do your best for the rest of this trip. Be a professional."

Before long, we're behind the scenes and Paige is interviewing models as they get ready. I'm sure no one but me could possibly guess how bummed she's feeling about being shut out of *Britain's Got Style* right now, because she's like her old self, smiling, passing out the compliments, and doing a magnificent job of saying the right thing to put others at ease. However, I suspect that if Paige acted like this all the time, our show would either be a huge hit or viewers would get tired of Pollyanna. Okay, I can't believe I actually just thought that. But, hey, I'm a realist.

Finally, it's time for the style show to start and we head

for our seats in the front row. But as I'm about to sit down, I notice a familiar name on the placard that's sitting on the empty seat next to Paige's chair. "Dylan Marceau is coming here tonight?" I exclaim as we sit down.

Paige gives me a nervous smile, then nods. But she looks too much like that proverbial canary-eating cat, and this makes me curious.

"How is that possible?"

She turns and peers at me. "What do you mean—how is *what* possible?"

"I mean why would Dylan be here?" Even though I'm confused, I realize I don't want to blow my cover. "He's not a British designer."

"Not all the shows this weekend are British designers," she reminds me.

"But he doesn't have a show here, does he?"

She shakes her head no. "But it's not out of the ordinary for a good designer to hop over the pond to check out the competition, Erin. London Fashion Week isn't that far away. Maybe Dylan wants to do some spying."

"Right . . ." I slowly nod, still taking this news in. "So where is he then?" I whisper as the lights go down and the music begins.

She shrugs then looks straight ahead. "I have no idea."

Then the show is about to begin and the amazing runway, which is actually multiple runways that resemble a maze, is suddenly flashing with colored lights and smoke and other special effects that make me feel slightly dizzy. The music is booming so loud it's like I can feel it pulsing through my veins. As I watch model after model parading some pretty extreme designs and strutting up, down, and all around this runway, I totally forget about Dylan's empty seat next to Paige.

Finally, the show ends and with my ears still ringing, I glance over to see that Paige looks disturbed.

"Are you okay?" I quietly ask. "Are you still upset about *Britian's Got Style?*"

She shrugs. "A little." Then she points to the empty seat next to her.

"Oh . . ." I nod. "Dylan didn't make it?"

With troubled eyes, she holds her chin up. "His flight was probably delayed."

"Yes." I nod in agreement. "Or he got stuck in London traffic."

Then, almost like magic, Paige puts on her sunny face, which has just a trace of sadness in it, and with JJ trailing her through the crowd, she launches into some off-the-cuff interviews with some of the glitterati in the British fashion world. I can't help but question Mark McCall's judgment. Can't he see that Paige is still a hot item over here? Our camera guys are hard-pressed to stick with her, so many fashionistas are glomming onto her. After about an hour, right as she's just finishing up with tonight's designer, I see Paige's eyes light up — like she's just spotted something over the designer's shoulder. Something I can't see. But Paige remains professional, wrapping up her interview with high praises to the designs and tonight's show. And that's when I see Dylan waving as he pushes his way toward her.

The next thing I know, Paige is in his arms and I'm just watching what looks like a scene in a movie — a final scene. Our camera guys are watching too — through their lenses. Although I suspect this is a scene that will end up on the cutting-room floor . . . or maybe not.

Chapter
19

I wasn't too surprised when Paige opted to let Dylan give her a ride back to the hotel. I didn't stay awake to make sure she got back at a decent hour either. Dylan is a good guy. He cares about Paige, and he's mature and trustworthy. Especially compared to Benjamin Kross. Really, compared to Benjamin, Dylan is a white knight in shining armor. And if his presence in London, if only for a few days, picks up Paige's spirits like this, well, who am I to complain?

But when Paige wakes me up at 6:48 on Saturday morning — a day when we weren't scheduled to go to "work" until noon — I feel a bit grumpy. "What's up?" I ask groggily, blinking at the light that's coming in through my opened shades.

"Sorry to wake you." Paige sits down on the edge of my bed . . . and suddenly I feel worried.

I sit up now and, rubbing the sleep from my eyes, I frown to see that Paige is still wearing that pretty peacock blue dress from last night. "Did you stay out all night?" I demand.

"Don't worry," she says with a smile that's even sunnier than yesterday's. "We didn't do anything you wouldn't approve of."

"How do you know what I would or wouldn't—"

"Never mind." She stands, strutting across the room like she's walking on a cloud.

"What is going on?" I ask as I crawl out of bed and walk over to look at her face. "Why are you so happy?"

She holds out her left hand and I feel a wave of shock and disbelief rush through me as I stare at what appears to be an engagement ring. "Please, Paige," I whisper, "tell me that's not what I think it is."

She nods and giggles. "It is!"

I sit down on the chair by the window and can only shake my head. How is this possible? Paige is barely twenty—how is it possible she is engaged? I feel slightly dizzy.

"I know you're shocked, Erin. But just be happy for me, okay? Last night was the most romantic night of my life. First of all, Dylan had hired a carriage ride that took us all through London—it was amazing and wonderful. And then he had arranged a midnight dinner, which was like something out of an old movie. Dylan has such a sweet old-world spirit." She sighs. "Then just after dessert was served, he pulled out a little blue box. Tiffany's blue." Paige sinks down into the chair across from me. "I thought I was going to faint when I saw it."

"And?" I try to make my face look happy, expectant, pleasant . . . but I feel like such a fake.

"And Dylan got down on one knee and told me that I was the love of his life and that he knew I was a little young, but that I would make him the happiest man in the world if I would agree to marry him."

"And you said yes." My voice sounds way too flat, but it's the best I can do.

"Of course." She holds out the ring again — like evidence. "Aren't you happy for me?"

I take in a long, slow breath. "I think I'm just in shock, Paige. It's a lot to take in. And it's so early." I stare at her in wonder. "Did you really stay out all night?"

"After he asked me, we were both too excited to call it a night. So we went dancing and had another carriage ride, then we walked along the river and talked and talked, and finally right after the sun came up, which was incredible, Dylan brought me back to the hotel."

"Wow ... you must be tired."

She sighs and nods. "I guess I'm tired ... but I might be too excited to sleep."

"You need to sleep, Paige. Today will be a long day." I take her by the arm, leading her back to her room and, as she continues to babble on about Dylan and how happy she is and how perfect this is, I help her out of her dress and into bed. "Just close your eyes," I say quietly. "Dream about Dylan."

She nods and smiles. "Yeah ... that's what I'll do."

After she's safely snuggled in, I go and put the Do Not Disturb sign on her door. Then I write a note that I slip under Fran's door explaining that Paige needs extra sleep this morning and shouldn't be awakened until noon. Today's first fashion show isn't until two, but there are three altogether and the last one won't be over until after ten. So if Paige wants to be in top form, she will need some rest. I'll leave it to Paige to tell Fran her news. How this will impact our show is anyone's guess. I'm just hoping that I still have time to secure a place in film school this coming fall. Because as I get dressed — and not very carefully — I am telling myself that I am almost finished with this rollercoaster ride called *On the Runway* with Paige Forrester.

With sunglasses on and a hat pulled low on my head, like I'm worried that I'll suddenly be the target of paparazzi—which is ridiculous—I walk through the hotel lobby and over to the restaurant where I had the good English breakfast a few days ago. Was it only a few days ago? But as I sit down and look over the menu, it occurs to me that I'm not really very hungry, and so I only order coffee and toast.

"No rashers?" the waiter asks hopefully.

I realize this is the same guy who waited on me before, the one I raved about the rashers to. "Sure," I tell him. "I'll have some rashers too."

He grins. "I saw you on television. Nicely done."

I smile and nod. "Thanks." *Yeah, nicely done*, I'm thinking. My big mouth about Paige's love life ignited this whole thing. As I eat I'm longing to talk to someone about what's going on. I consider Mom, but know that Paige should be the one to tell her. Then I think of Mollie, but I don't totally trust Mollie not to go public with this. Finally, I decide to tell Blake. He's been a good one to keep confidences before.

So after I leave the restaurant, I go outside and hit speed dial for Blake's cell phone. I have no idea what time it is in LA, but I'm desperate.

"Hey," Blake says in a congenial tone, "How's London, Erin?"

"Oh, it's so good to hear your voice." I tell him about how Paige was uninvited from *Britian's Got Style*. "She took it pretty hard."

"That's too bad," he says. "So how's everything else going? You girls have sure been getting a lot of press."

"Even back home?" Maybe I should pay more attention to this gossip thing.

"This is LA, Erin."

"Oh, yeah."

"So, really, what's the story on Paige's mystery man?"

I take a second before I respond. "You heard that too?"

"Oh, yeah ... it's the talk of the town."

"Well, can I totally trust you?"

"Of course. But hang on a minute, okay?"

"Sure." So I wait for what is actually about a minute, then Blake is back.

"Sorry about that," he tells me. "I was with Ben."

"You were with Ben?"

"Yeah. He's kinda bummed about Paige. He asked me to hang with him. And, hey, at least I'm keeping him from a bad night of clubbing."

"What time is it there, anyway?"

"A little past midnight."

"Oh ... right."

"So what's up?"

In one long rambling sentence, I tell him about Paige's engagement.

"Wow." He lets out a long sigh.

"I know ... wow. I'm still in shock. I mean, she's not much older than me. And there's the show. I just can't believe it."

"Is she happy?"

I consider this. "Yeah, she's like over-the-moon happy."

"Good for her."

"Really?" I consider his point. "You think this is a good thing?"

"Well, if she's happy, how can I not be happy for her? Dylan is a good guy."

"Yeah ... I guess."

"But you're not happy for her?"

"I just feel caught, Blake. Like I've been so jerked around in this show. I've given up a lot. Now it's like the show is going to go straight down the drain."

"Just because Paige is engaged?"

I think about that. "Yeah, maybe I am overreacting."

"Seriously, you don't think they'll run off and get married and just give up their careers, do you?" He chuckles. "I'm guessing they'll have a long engagement."

"You could be right." Suddenly I feel a bit hopeful.

"And, really, what good does it do for you to be bummed, Erin? It's Paige's life, right? As her sister all you can do is support her and love her. You, of all people, should know that she makes her own choices."

"You're right, Blake." I let out a relieved sigh. "I knew I would feel better talking to you."

"Really?"

"Yeah. You almost always make me feel better."

"I like the sound of that."

"Okay, now remember to not breathe a word of this to anyone yet."

"I promise."

"I'm sure Paige will break the news soon enough." I wince at the thought.

"Poor Ben."

"I know. But I'm sure he'll get over her."

Blake doesn't say anything in response.

"Anyway, like you said, there's nothing we can do about it," I add, a bit awkwardly.

"Yes. That's right. I'll be praying for Paige and Dylan ... and you too. Although I was doing that anyway."

I thank him and we hang up, and I realize that he really is right: There's nothing I can do about this anyway. I might as well be happy for Paige. And really, isn't this better than seeing her all depressed over the *Britain's Got Style* rejection? Then I remember how Jesus said we should rejoice with those who rejoice, and right now my sister is rejoicing. So I will join her!

I decide to stop at a bakery not far from the hotel and buy a chocolate torte for my sister. (Hopefully, in her happy state, she won't think about the calories.) The baker uses pink frosting to write Dylan & Paige and frames it in a heart. Then I go back to my room and prepare myself to wait until noon. But as I wait, I pray. I ask God to help me to be supportive and positive about this new era of Paige's life. I ask him to help me to trust him more for my own life — knowing that no matter what my sister does, it's God's direction that should lead me. And finally I ask him to bless my sister and Dylan.

It's about eleven thirty when I hear a tapping at the adjoining door. I go and get my celebratory cake and open the door with a big smile.

"Is that for me?" Paige asks happily.

"Yeah. I thought we should celebrate."

"Oh, Erin." Paige takes the cake, sets it on a side table, then gives me a big, hard hug. "Thank you!"

"I'm sorry I wasn't more excited earlier," I say as I get the cake and follow her into the suite. "I was in shock and not quite awake."

"I know," she says as she gets out plates and forks from the kitchenette and I start a pot of coffee. "I should've broken it to you a bit more gently. But I was so excited. I couldn't wait another minute."

"I understand. I mean, I saw how much you brightened up yesterday ... after Dylan called."

"So you knew he called?"

I chuckle. "Yeah. He and I had a little chat yesterday — after he heard about my little press conference."

"It's funny — I was mad at you for saying that. But now ... well, I'm so happy."

I slice into the cake, putting a big piece on Paige's plate. "So when are you guys going to announce this publicly?"

She forks into the torte. "Probably today. No sense in waiting ... because with my luck, someone probably knows now anyway."

We talk about the logistics of this new development as we eat our chocolate torte. Then as Paige is pouring us some coffee, she turns to me. "I'll need you more than ever now, Erin."

I laugh. "You'll need me?"

"Dylan and I talked about this. He thinks I need to share more of the show with you, Erin, and I think he's right."

Dylan is growing on me more and more. "So you plan to continue with the show?"

"For now I do."

I slowly nod. "Do you have any idea when you'll actually get married?"

"Of course, we haven't set the date. If Dylan had his way, which he says he won't push for, it would be next week."

"Seriously?"

Paige nods with sparkling eyes.

"But how about you?" I ask.

She shrugs. "I'm not really sure. I definitely need at least a year to plan a fantastic wedding."

"And you'd continue with the show throughout that year?"

"Well, we are under contract, Erin."

"But we both know contracts can be broken."

"Yes, Dylan pointed that out." Her smile gets even bigger, if that's possible. "Which reminds me of something."

"What?"

"Fran called this morning. It seems Mark McCall is rethinking his decision about having me on his show."

"Really?"

"Fran said that Helen is putting some pressure on his boss. Now there's a possibility we will do his show after all."

I look at the clock and realize we were originally scheduled to start the show today. "Then we better get busy to make it there—"

"Not here in London, Erin."

"Huh?"

"In the Bahamas."

"The Bahamas?"

Her eyes sparkle as she grins. "Yes. How cool would that be?" Then she explains that the Bahamas trip will be scheduled after we get back home.

"So we are going to be busy." I study her closely. "And you're okay with that ... I mean, in light of this engagement biz?"

"I think so. I think I'll take Dylan's advice too."

"What advice?"

"Remember I told you that Dylan thinks you should be more involved in the show, Erin? The more I think about it, the more I think he's right. If you stepped up more ... I might be able to step back a little."

Okay, I've been down this road before, but I'm not going to say that. "So you think you're really ready to share the spotlight with me now?"

She nods. "I really do. I was silly and selfish to try to hog it all to myself. Look where it got me — I almost had a complete breakdown."

"It's not like they can ever use me to replace you," I remind her. "*On the Runway* is what it is because of you, Paige. But I could help to share the load a little more."

"And you don't mind?" She sets down her fork and looks into my eyes. "I mean, I'm not stupid, Erin. I know this was never your dream. I don't want to feel like I'm dragging you along against your will."

"I'll admit I've been kind of grumpy … especially when I'm not quite sure what my role is. But I actually enjoyed doing those interviews after you broke down. When I'm allowed to be myself, it's kind of fun."

She looks relieved. "So maybe we can do this? I can be engaged and we can still do a first-rate show?"

"I don't see why not."

"Because I really do love Dylan, Erin. If I had to choose between him and the show, I would choose Dylan."

I smile as I raise a forkful of chocolate torte in a toast. "Here's to you and Dylan, Paige. May God bless you both!"

She has tears in her eyes. "Thanks." She lifts her fork again. "And here's to sisters sticking together through thick and thin." She looks down at what little is left of her cake and giggles. "And if I keep eating this, I'll be more thick than thin."

I laugh and hold up my fork. "Here's to sisters! Sisters forever!"

We click forks and as I take a bite I know that somehow, some way, and with God's help — despite obstacles of competition, jealousy, misunderstanding, and all the other challenges of sisterhood — Paige and I really will be sisters forever.

Check out this excerpt from book five in the On the Runway series

A NOVEL

Glamour

On the Runway

Melody Carlson

Bestselling Author

Chapter

1

After nearly six months of the drama and chaos connected to it, I hoped we'd finally left the reality show *Malibu Beach* behind. Far behind. And really, it seemed a natural assumption. Especially after Paige permanently distanced herself from one of the show's ex-stars, Benjamin Kross, by getting engaged to brilliant young designer Dylan Marceau last month in London. Apparently I was wrong.

It turns out that *Malibu Beach* is the reality show that keeps on giving. And now they want us to "give us the opportunity" to devote an entire *On the Runway* episode to one of their popular stars, Brogan Braxton. Brogan, who is only nineteen, recently declared herself a fashion expert, and is now coming out with a new line of beach clothing called The BBB (aka Brogan Braxton Beachwear).

"But these are awful," Paige tells our producer, Helen Hudson, as we all lean forward to peer at the images on the screen of Fran's laptop computer.

"I have to admit I'm with my sister on this one," I tell

them. "What made Brogan Braxton suddenly decide she was a designer?"

"You mean besides Daddy's wallet?" Paige teases.

"I think you're missing the point," Fran says as she closes the laptop.

Helen adjusts her glasses and clears her throat. "Brogan is still one of the hottest commodities in the teen market."

Fran waves a piece of paper. "According to this, Brogan has almost as many Facebook friends as Ellen DeGeneres."

"Yes, and they're *real* friends too." I roll my eyes. I may be the last person on this continent to join Facebook, but I'm still holding out.

"I consider my Facebook friends to be real," Paige says to me in a slightly wounded way.

"Yes, and I'm sure they'd still be your friends if you didn't have a show, right?" I turn back to Helen. She's encouraging me to take a bigger role in our show and I am trying. "But I thought we were talking about fashion, and I still don't get Brogan Braxton, or The BBB . . . which, by the way, also stands for the Better Business Bureau, and I wonder how they feel about—"

"You're missing the point," Fran says with a bit of aggravation.

"Remember the *R* word, girls?" Helen asks in a slightly bored tone.

"Ratings." Paige sighs. "Never mind whether it's fashionable or not, as long as the viewers tune in."

"Wait a minute," I say. "Just because we feature a fashion designer doesn't mean we have to approve of their style, does it?"

"That's true." Paige nods. "And my fans expect me to be honest. Do you have a problem if we do the show and I express my candid opinions about The BBB?"

Helen shrugs, then pushes her chair away from the conference table. "Just keep the fans happy, Paige. Keep the ratings up." She stands and peers down at her. "And keep it clean."

"Oh, you know I always keep it clean, Helen." Paige flashes her best smile.

Helen reaches down and pats Paige's cheek. "Yes, darling, but you know what I mean. Keep it polite and respectable. You have an image to maintain. One element that makes *On the Runway* different from the other shows is that Paige Forrester, for the most part, is a lady. And the sponsors seem to appreciate that."

"You don't ask for much," Fran says to Helen. "Just keep the ratings up and play nice. That's so easy to do."

"Yes, well, our Paige is quite expert at it." Helen laughs as she heads for the door. "Sorry to meet and run, girls, but I have a major appointment with the network in about ten minutes. Ta-ta!"

Fran shuffles some papers into a stack, then slides them over to her assistant, Leah. "Brogan's show is scheduled for this Saturday at two." Fran gets a worried look. "That's not your mom's wedding date, is it?"

"No, that's the following weekend," Paige says. "You are coming, aren't you?"

"Yes, of course, I already RSVP'd. I just blanked it." Fran takes a long drink from her bottle of water.

"The crew is scheduled already," Leah fills in for her. "You girls can come to wardrobe around ten then we'll head over to the site and do the pre-show shoot. After the fashion show, we'll do the wrap-up." Leah smiles. "The usual stuff."

I'm curious as to why Leah is telling us this … since it's what Fran usually does. Maybe Leah, like me, is trying to take a more active role in the show.

"Brogan wants to do an interview before the show," Fran says, then looks at Leah. "When was that scheduled?"

"She asked for Wednesday afternoon," Leah tells us. "Two o'clock … on *Malibu Beach* turf."

"So Brogan called us and asked us to interview her?" Paige frowns.

"Her people called us," Leah clarifies.

"We thought we might get something to use for the show," Fran says.

"And the interview is just with Brogan?" Paige asks. "Not any of the other cast members or the *Malibu Beach* crew, right?"

"I'm not totally sure about that," Fran tells her. "In fact, it sounds as if their crew will be filming this too. Just in case it's show-worthy."

"You mean in case they want to *make* it show-worthy." Paige groans. "Something about this whole thing is starting to smell fishy. It's not some kind of setup to get me, is it?"

"No, of course not." Fran shakes her head.

"Because I know Brogan was pretty close with Mia Renwick. I mean, they weren't *best* friends. But when Mia died in that car accident after the Oscars, it was like everyone in the cast suddenly decided they had been her very best friends. And I can understand that. But I also understand that some of those girls seriously hate me, Fran."

"At least you're not with Ben now," I remind her.

"And I hear he's getting back with Waverly Stratton,"

Leah says in a somewhat-gossipy tone. "I saw it on *WWW* last weekend."

"The world wide web?" I ask.

Leah laughs. "No, that new entertainment show, *Who's Who and Why*. Haven't you seen it?"

I shake my head, thinking maybe it should be called *Who's Who and Who Cares*?

"Really, Erin," she tells me, "you need to keep up. Anyway, they showed some pics of Waverly and Benjamin at a club, and in the interview Waverly said that they were together."

Paige looks skeptical. "That was a stretch on Waverly's part."

"So back to the topic at hand." Fran taps her pen impatiently. "What exactly are you saying, Paige? That you don't want to work with Brogan?"

"I just don't want to be sabotaged and end up on their show looking like an evil backstabbing witch, like the time Mia and Ben set me up on their show after the dating scandal."

"Seriously, Paige, what could they actually do?" I ask her. "If it starts to go sideways, we'll just walk out." I turn to Fran. "Right?"

She nods then takes another sip of water.

"Speaking of walking out ..." Leah holds up her Black-Berry. "Don't you need to get moving, Paige? I have you scheduled for that spot on *ET* this afternoon, remember?"

Paige suddenly stands. "That's right."

"Why don't you let me drive you?" Leah offers. "That way you can get ready on the way over there. And we'll be on time."

"Great idea." Paige reaches in her bag and then tosses me her car keys. "Guess I'll see you at home." And just like that they are gone.

I turn to Fran and study her for a moment.

"*What?*" she says in a slightly cranky tone.

"Are you ... *okay?*" I use what I hope is a gentle voice.

She shrugs and reaches for her bag. "I'm fine." We both get up, but before we leave the conference room I decide to try again.

"Really, Fran, you don't seem like yourself. Is something bothering you?"

And just like that, like I pressed the wrong button, she starts to crumble. Tears are coming and her hands are shaking and I wonder if I should've kept my big mouth closed. Just the same, I go over and close the blinds on the glass door and ask her to sit back down. "What's wrong?" I ask.

"I didn't want anyone to know—to know—that—" She chokes in a sob.

"Know *what?*" I'm seriously worried now. Something is really wrong.

She looks at me with watery eyes. "My cancer is back."

I blink. "You had cancer?"

"Had ... and now I have it again."

I reach out and put my hand on her arm. "Oh, Fran."

"I was diagnosed with leukemia in my early thirties. I went through all the treatment and it seemed to have worked. I thought it was gone. And now I have it again."

"I'm so sorry."

She nods as she opens her bag and retrieves a packet of tissues, pulls one out, then wipes her eyes. "I'd been in remission for almost six years. Six years!" She blows her nose. "And five years is considered cured. I really I believed I was cured."

"But you're getting treatment?"

"I started chemo last Friday."

"Does Helen know?"

Fran shakes her head. "No one knows. Today I told Leah I was feeling under the weather so that she could help me out in the meeting."

"I wondered why she was so involved."

"But I don't know if I can hide it for the whole time ... I mean, while I'm doing chemo."

I don't know what to say. I've never known anyone with cancer before.

"Promise me you won't tell anyone," she begs. "I wouldn't have told you, Erin, except you pushed me. And I trust you. Just promise you won't tell."

I nod. "Sure, it's not my place to talk about your personal life to anyone."

"I want to be realistic, and if I can't do my job ... well, I will deal with that when the time comes." She gives me a forced-looking smile. "But my oncologist was quite positive. She says the new drugs are better than before. And she really thinks the chemo will wipe it out again."

"But doesn't chemo kind of wipe a person out too?" I ask. "I mean, how can you expect to work while you're going through treatment?" I don't point out that, even today, she seemed wasted—and she's barely begun her chemo.

"My doctor seemed to think it's a possibility. A lot of people continue with their jobs during treatment. There are some new anti-nausea meds that are supposed to work. I just have to take it easy, get lots of rest, drink water, eat the right foods."

"Oh ..." I'm trying to absorb this. But it just doesn't make sense. I always assumed if a person had cancer, they needed time off ... to get treatment and recover.

"I *have* to work, Erin." Her eyes look desperate now. "Not just financially, because I know insurance will help. But work is my life. And without it, I wouldn't have a chance of surviving this. Can you *understand* that?"

"I guess so." Although I silently question how or why work should be anyone's life. "But, as your friend, I want you to do whatever it takes to get well. That's the important thing. Can you understand *that*?"

Fran smiles. "You're such a good kid, Erin."

I kind of shrug. "Yeah, well . . ."

"Not that you're such a kid. You're mature for your age, and you have a really good head on your shoulders. And I know I can trust you with this."

"Of course."

"And I want to go to the Bahamas with you girls on the upcoming shoot. I've really been looking forward to it. And I don't know what I'd do if I missed out on that . . ." She looks close to tears again. "It would feel like . . . like the cancer had won."

I take in a slow breath. "Then you have to do everything you can to get well." I think about the timeline. "But that gives you less than four weeks. Can you be healthy enough to travel by then?"

"That's my goal."

"And you wouldn't go if your doctor recommended against it?"

She pauses as if considering. "No, of course not. That would be foolish."

"If there's anything I can do to help," I offer, "please, feel free to ask. And I mean that, Fran. I wouldn't say it if I didn't mean it."

"Thanks, Erin. I believe you. And I'll keep that in mind."
She turns to me with a funny grin. "So, how are you at holding a girlfriend's hair back while she worships at the porcelain throne?"

"Huh?"

She chuckles. "You never were a party girl, were you?"

"Not so much."

Now she pats my shoulder. "One of the things I admire about you. You are *so you*." She slowly stands. "I think I need to get home now . . . I need to get some rest."

We walk out to the parking lot together and, although Fran is quiet, my brain is buzzing like a mosquito on caffeine. And whether it makes sense or not, I am suddenly feeling very responsible. Not only for Fran's wellbeing and medical treatment, but for how it might impact our show if she's trying to direct us when she really should be home in bed. It's got me very worried and I really think Helen should be informed. And yet I know I have to keep my promise to Fran.

"You take care now," I say as I wait for her to get into her car. "Promise you'll call me if you need anything."

She gives me a weak smile as she puts her window down. "Yeah. And you promise not to worry about me. Okay?"

I nod, knowing that's a promise I might not be able to keep.

"Leah will call you with the details on the interview with Brogan. And I'll see you on Wednesday."

"Get some rest," I say as her window goes up. She makes another weak smile, then drives away. And suddenly I feel like crying. *Poor Fran!* Why is this happening to her? But instead of breaking down right here in the parking lot, I slowly walk over to Paige's car, and as I walk, I pray. I ask God to do a miracle in Fran's life. I'm not exactly sure what kind of a miracle I have in mind; I'm trusting that God knows what's best. But that's what I'm expecting—a real true honest-to-goodness miracle.

DISCUSSION QUESTIONS FOR
SPOTLIGHT

1. In this story, Erin is thrust further into the world of fashion and the drama that surrounds it. How would you handle the pressures of navigating this unfamiliar world and dealing with a high-maintenance sister?

2. Erin goes from being behind the camera to taking a more prominent role on the show. If you were Erin, would you have gladly accepted this role? Or would you have tried harder to stay behind the scenes? Why?

3. If you were Erin, how would you treat Paige in this book? Do you think Erin sacrifices too much for her sister? What do you think of their relationship?

4. Mollie goes through a tough time accepting the prospect of being a single mother and has parents who don't always support her. If you were her friend, what would you have done or said?

5. Paige and Erin make a pact to swear off boys at this point in their careers, yet Paige publicly breaks the pact several times. If you'd made this pact with Paige, what would be your reaction to her behavior?

6. Erin is promised a segment on On the Runway that will deal with body image and eating disorders. If you had a chance, would you do a segment on this topic? If not, what topic would you choose for your segment?

7. Mollie follows the tabloids and Internet gossip while Erin does not. Which person do you most relate to? Why?

8. In the quiz Erin and Paige take on the flight to London, which animal do you think you would be? Why? Do you

have any "peacocks" in your life? How do you tend to treat them?

9. When Erin is on the Shakespeare tour in London, a woman named Mildred claims she would "rather spend money on those nice clothes than the horrid rags" her granddaughter used to wear, even though the "nice clothes" cost a lot. Do you agree with Mildred? Is good fashion worth the high price?

10. Paige craves publicity throughout most of the book, until she realizes there is such a thing as bad publicity, and then panics. If you were Paige, how would you have reacted to all the negative comments?

11. Much of the book focuses on body image and the thinness of models, and at one point both Paige and Erin agree the fashion industry promotes thinness as the best way to look good in clothes. Do you ever feel the pressure to look a certain way? How have you dealt with this pressure?

12. Erin gives a very detailed description of how Barbie would look if she were real. Describe your reaction after reading that segment. Do the facts make you look at Barbie—and our culture—differently?

13. Has this book affected the way you look at the fashion industry? If so, how?

14. What was your reaction to Paige and Dylan's sudden engagement? Do you think Paige is ready to get married? Why do you think Paige is in love with Dylan?

15. Erin discovers she really likes British style. What are your favorite styles or designers? Does anyone influence your own style? If so, why do you think that is?

16. Have your feelings toward Benjamin changed since the first book? How?

On the Runway
from Melody Carlson

When Paige and Erin Forrester are offered their own TV show,
sisterly bonds are tested as the girls learn that it takes two to keep
their once-in-a-lifetime project afloat.

Premiere
Book One

Catwalk
Book Two

Rendezvous
Book Three

Spotlight
Book Four

Carter House Girls Series
from Melody Carlson

Mix six teenage girls and one '60s fashion icon (retired, of course) in an old Victorian-era boarding home. Add boys and dating, a little high-school angst, and throw in a Kate Spade bag or two ... and you've got the Carter House Girls, Melody Carlson's chick lit series for young adults!

Mixed Bags

Book One

Stealing Bradford

Book Two

Homecoming Queen

Book Three

Viva Vermont!

Book Four

Lost in Las Vegas

Book Five

New York Debut

Book Six

Spring Breakdown

Book Seven

Last Dance

Book Eight

Pick up a copy today at your favorite bookstore!

Visit www.zondervan.com/teen

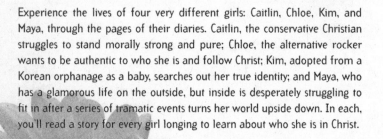
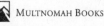

Share Your Thoughts

With the Author: Your comments will be forwarded to the author when you send them to *zauthor@zondervan.com*.

With Zondervan: Submit your review of this book by writing to *zreview@zondervan.com*.

Free Online Resources at
www.zondervan.com

Zondervan AuthorTracker: Be notified whenever your favorite authors publish new books, go on tour, or post an update about what's happening in their lives at www.zondervan.com/authortracker.

Daily Bible Verses and Devotions: Enrich your life with daily Bible verses or devotions that help you start every morning focused on God. Visit www.zondervan.com/newsletters.

Free Email Publications: Sign up for newsletters on Christian living, academic resources, church ministry, fiction, children's resources, and more. Visit www.zondervan.com/newsletters.

Zondervan Bible Search: Find and compare Bible passages in a variety of translations at www.zondervanbiblesearch.com.

Other Benefits: Register yourself to receive online benefits like coupons and special offers, or to participate in research.

ZONDERVAN®

ZONDERVAN.com/
AUTHORTRACKER
follow your favorite authors